BY FLOWER AND DEAN STREET

Patrice Chaplin is an author, playwright, journalist and the producer of the BBC radio documentary on 'The Cabala in Spain'. In addition to seven novels, including *Harriet Hunter, Having it Away* and *The Unforgotten*, she has written many short stories and plays for radio and television. She is the author of *From the Balcony* for the National Theatre and Radio 3. Her novel *Siesta*, which is based on the years described in her volume of autobiography, *Albany Park*, has recently been filmed. Her latest book is *Another City*, a sequel to *Albany Park*.

PATRICE CHAPLIN

By Flower and Dean Street
&
The Love Apple

A Methuen Paperback

A Methuen Paperback

BY FLOWER AND DEAN STREET

First published in 1976 by
Gerald Duckworth & Co Ltd
This edition published 1988
by Methuen London Ltd
A Division of OPG Services Limited
Michelin House, 81 Fulham Road, London SW3 6RB
Copyright © 1976 Patrice Chaplin

Printed and bound in Great Britain
by Cox & Wyman Ltd, Reading

British Library Cataloguing in Publication Data

Chaplin, Patrice
By. Flower and Dean Street ; &, The love apple
I. Title
823'.914 [F]

ISBN 0 413 18820 5

BY FLOWER AND DEAN STREET

1

The London sky was pale and hard and glistened like an ice rink. At the end of a long wintry front garden stood a narrow three-storey house with dry dignified trees on either side. Everything was still. The two lower floors were brightly lit and at some windows curtains weren't drawn. Light from the street lamp didn't reach the garden because rough overgrown shrubs with dead honeysuckle tangling through them ganged together just inside the railings, and small ones, spiky, treacherous, hid by the gate. A child's new tricycle lay on its side across the path, its handlebars poking into the cracked earth of the flower border. A wind shook the trees. Then everything was still again.

A light went off on the first floor. The front door opened, and a man and woman walked quickly along the path. 'Damn the child!' the man said and swung the tricycle away across the lawn and into a shed while the woman went on to the gate, the gravel spitting under her tall elegant shoes. She waited on the pavement, her black fur coat sleek around her, and the light of the street lamp shone on her face, pale and beautiful, as she turned and shouted, 'Daniel! We're late.' From the road, the house no longer looked isolated — there were other houses nearby, a church hung over the garden shed, cars lined the kerb.

Daniel ran to the gate, out of breath, and, knowing the plants well, jumped to avoid them. But sly, undercover, they were waiting somewhere else, and he tripped and swore.

'I'll pull them up tomorrow, Connie,' he promised.

He closed the gate. It squeaked open immediately and they got into the car.

'Why doesn't he put it away I wonder? Does he want to get it pinched?' 'Perhaps he does.' She laughed. 'I think he's bored with it already and daren't admit it.'

He started the engine, and then turned and kissed her. 'I didn't give you this in front of the children.' He took a small black case from his pocket. 'I wanted to wait until we were alone. A little extra present.'

She opened the case. Glittering on a nest of black satin was a small diamond brooch shaped like a heart. Still smiling, she said, 'Oh. Oh, it's lovely, Daniel. Really lovely.' She was all the more touched as once again he'd given her something she would never use. She never wore brooches — thought they were for elderly women. It would join the bottles of scent, kid gloves, jewelled powder compacts, which were aging elegantly in her bedroom. 'But why a heart?'

He squeezed her hand. The car moved forward, and she undid the fur and pinned the heart to her dress.

Silence came back into the long wintry garden and the narrow house looked lonely again.

It was Connie's thirtieth birthday.

2

The restaurant was well known for its intimate atmosphere, its roast beef, its blazing log-fire and the difficulty of getting a table.

They sat with two friends by the fire as the waiter cleared the empty Beaujolais bottle and glasses and brought the champagne. Jane had black bright eyes. She was full of energy, and she considered herself Connie's best friend. She pushed back her long shining hair and started on her third portion of fresh figs.

'Can't get enough of them,' she said, and seeing Daniel laughing at her, wriggled athletically. She could never keep still.

Her husband, Mark, was quiet and withdrawn and had pale, powdery skin like a moth.

Daniel raised his glass. 'Happy Birthday, and thank you for ten marvellous years.'

'They haven't all been marvellous,' said Connie. 'What about when I couldn't cook? You can't have forgotten that. Are you drunk? It got better when I learned to open tins.' She laughed, and her teeth were slightly protruding; but even that, Jane thought, seemed attractive on Connie. 'Before that, poor man! The burnt dinners, undercooked dinners, non-existent dinners he had to come home to.'

'You're exaggerating,' said Mark mournfully. 'I've had some very good dinners at your place.' He always seemed tired except when he talked about his work.

'They were usually burnt and undercooked at the same time,' murmured Connie.

'It's lovely,' said Jane, flinging her hair back into the eyes of a passing waiter and nearly toppling his tray. She shivered towards the next table. 'I haven't had champagne for ages.'

Her black plain dress, its material, its style, seemed only to emphasise her flat chest. 'It's as much as I can do to get Mark to remember my birthday, let alone celebrate.' She looked at Connie's bosom, generously revealed by the cut-out in the bodice of her dark-red dress, and she had to admit that in spite of nursing four children, it was still shapely. Jane gulped some champagne. 'That's a super brooch.'

The cut-out was shaped like a diamond; and Mark, eyeing more than the brooch, said, 'Diamonds are definitely the evening's motif.' Something like light came back into his eyes.

'The frock was meant to be modest,' Daniel told him. 'But the long sleeves and high neck obviously got too much for the designer, so he ripped it open at the most telling point.'

'You need something super when you get into your thirties,' said Connie. 'Thirty! Definitely the end. No more silly girlish indulgences—eh, Papa?' She pulled Daniel's ear. 'Can't blame my mistakes on immaturity.' Her voice was husky.

'Will you have any more kids?' asked Jane. 'God, that sounds awful. I didn't mean they're a mistake.'

'When David's at school, perhaps. I'd like one more baby. I'd like really to enjoy it, lavish attention on it.' Her eyes were warm, caressing, as she smiled. Connie looked at people as though she cared for them; she'd been well-loved. She twisted the glass round, and the champagne splashed about and fizzed, and Jane noticed that even her hands were rounded and in proportion. 'I had the others in such a rush. There was so much to do. I couldn't give them enough time.'

'I'm certainly not having any more,' said Jane defiantly, and she looked at Daniel, for some reason, as though he'd contradict her.

He didn't. 'It's the only solution,' he said firmly. 'They're easy to build, economical, hygienic—they're sensible.'

'What's he on about?' asked Jane. 'Not tower blocks again?'

'They suck up the drifting surplus overnight. You can cram fifty families in the space you would use for one. They might not be pretty,' he added sharply, as though Mark had opposed him, 'But how pretty is half a million with nowhere to live?'

'He's going grey,' said Jane.

'Who?' asked Connie.

'Daniel. And his stomach! It's a hazard.'

'You ought to see the ones the Council get. You'd soon forget your preoccupation with saving cornices and low-timbered roofs.'

Mark didn't answer. His cheeks full of unchewed food, he looked like a hamster.

'Panoico. That whole group are panoico, Mark. What do they know about housing women and kids?'

'How d'you mean, a hazard?' asked Connie.

'Well, it sticks out,' said Jane.

Connie looked at Daniel's stomach. 'You mean someone might bump into it?' she giggled.

'No. It's a health hazard. Men over a certain age should watch it. I'd stop giving him puddings.'

'You might say the hospital dominates the heath. You might say it should have been spread across, rather than up — but it saved space, for crissake, Mark. It's economical.'

Mark still didn't answer. Then he remembered the forgotten food and started chewing.

'Do you know you can see it from wherever you are on the heath?' said Jane disingenuously. 'Even in the woody bits.'

Not quite sure of her tone, Daniel looked at her, his dark eyes, with their yellow lights, unblinking.

'I mean, wherever you are in Hampstead you just never forget that hospital.'

'People need clean, hygienic blocks,' he said swiftly and refilled the glasses. 'Anyway, Mark, how's Golders Green's next best thing to a Regency terrace working out?'

Connie nudged him.

'It's not!' snapped Jane.

'The builders are no good,' said Mark gently. 'Very expensive, unreliable —'

'And who's to blame for that?' asked Jane. 'Who chose them?' Smiling, Mark pointed at himself.

'Change them,' said Daniel.

He started to answer, but Jane said: 'It's been unlucky from the start, that scheme. He did the drawings and spec. in his spare time. Then he found he'd put the drawings back to front. They'd all have been peeing in the front garden.'

Daniel looked sympathetically at the younger man and thought of a way to change the subject, so that Jane would keep out of it. 'There's another council meeting Friday. I'm

7

proposing new flats for that old station site near—'

'Oh no,' said Jane flatly. 'Don't get him involved in any more work. I hardly—'

'—Camden Town. I think we should use a local architect. You'll have to do some provisional drawings.' His decisive tone dropped under Jane's high howl and gave Mark confidence to reply, softly, 'I'll have to think about it.'

'I hardly ever see him as it is.' Jane bounced up and down in her chair.

'Have some more figs,' said Daniel.

Mark suddenly looked crushed by fatigue. Jane took his energy, absorbed it and shone even brighter, spoke even louder, her smiles thrusting, her eyes jabbing, leaving him shrunken and uninteresting at the tail end of everyone's conversation. She took the glow from everything except Connie. She even took it away from the brass ornaments round the fire.

Almost before Daniel looked in his direction, the waiter was beside him and another bottle was whisked to the table.

'It may be unimaginative, even ugly,' said Daniel. 'No. Not ugly, I'd call it uncompromising. It serves a damn useful purpose. It's a million times more efficient than that old Victorian one.'

'Efficient?' cried Jane. 'Hell. It took me half an hour just to find the X-Ray department. There's no signs anywhere. Even the nurses don't know where anything is. I walked miles. It's like a city.'

'When I look back on my twentieth birthday—help!' said Connie. 'I thought leaving your teens was the end of the world. I cried. D'you remember, Daniel? I've led a very sheltered life, when I think about it.'

'It's been uneventful compared with everyone else's,' said Jane, and she stared at Daniel. 'I mean, it's been so smooth. Married straight from boarding school—'

'Well, so were you,' said Mark.

'No. It's different. I mean—' For a moment she looked sad, and as her eyes were pointing at the empty plate Daniel was going to suggest yet another helping of figs, when she said suddenly, 'I'm going to teach full-time. I've decided. The money's not worth it doing just mornings.'

8

'Oh no,' said Daniel. 'That means you'll be even fitter, your cheeks will be even rosier. You're already the healthiest Mum in N.W.3. Do you know that?' He leaned towards her, playfully. She turned scarlet. 'You'll put us all to shame.' He straightened back into his chair.

'I'll give them isometrics and more running,' she said breathlessly. 'Running's what they need.'

Mark pointed over Daniel's shoulder and Daniel turned round quickly.

'What?' He frowned, seeing nothing sensational.

'Through the windows, across the road—one of the most beautiful houses in London. Keats House. Late eighteenth century. Surrounded by gardens. Don't you just long to tear it down and build one of your nice gleaming tower blocks?'

Daniel stared at him—at his long floppy face which strain and living with Jane had made already old, at his blue, harmless eyes, his woman's mouth—and he said, 'I'd really love you for the new project. If you can get it. I'll certainly push you. We need an architect with taste.'

'Yes but—' Jane exploded.

'You'll get a good fee,' he added quickly, not quite looking at Jane.

'How much?' she asked.

He shrugged. 'Double, treble what—'

'We'll think about it,' she decided. 'I need a new fridge.'

'No more for me.' Mark put his hand over his glass and tried not to yawn.

'Don't you ever get bored, Connie? Honestly?' asked Jane.

Connie, surprised, shook her head.

'You look all right, though. I don't know how you do it with four kids and that big house. What's your secret? Vitamin E?'

Connie laughed, and the way she looked at Daniel suggested he had a lot to do with it.

Mark was saying, 'With the prices of everything now you can't afford them.'

'Can't afford what?' asked Jane.

'Kids.'

'Well, you're not having any more, so don't start worrying your head about affording them.' Her long teeth gleamed as she smiled at Connie. 'He can't even cope with one.'

'We've enough difficulty with one,' Mark was saying.

'But you've put your money into the cottage and you've had some rather exclusive holidays,' said Daniel.

'Jane likes to feel free.'

'Free!' Jane crossed her eyes.

Daniel put his glass down and his hand dropped out of sight. Suddenly Connie looked flushed — pleased. Daniel's eyes were hot as he watched her.

Aroused, Jane could only wriggle wildly. Connie shivered a little, as though with anticipation. Nobody saw it, except Jane.

'Is that beauty spot by your eye real?' she asked fiercely.

'I hope so,' murmured Connie, her mind not really on what Jane was saying.

'Mark, d'you hear that? Mark!' she cried; and a waiter crept up, wondering how to deal with this obtrusive customer without upsetting her host, whom he cherished for his demeanour, his reckless appetite and his bank balance. He offered her more champagne, naively thinking that that would shut her up. After several of her more spectacular sounds, she dragged Mark's attention from out of whatever private grey crevice it had been hiding in. 'Yes?' he sighed.

'D'you know that Connie's beauty spot is real? I always thought it was false.'

'Is it?' he replied. Nothing much of what his wife said ever got through to him.

'I like this place better than the one we went to on Connie's last birthday. It's more intimate.'

Mark's empty expression suggested that it was too intimate for him with her at the same table. Her remarks whizzed wall to wall like a ball on a squash court. Her 'Oh gosh's' and 'How terrific's' became part of other people's conversations. Her shriek, as the third bottle was uncorked, had everyone frozen.

'Daniel gave me a velvet dress — you know, one of those lovely new Ossie Clark ones — as well as this brooch.' Connie lowered her voice dramatically, hoping she'd follow her example. 'The children gave me an electric mixer.'

'I thought you'd already got a mixer.'

'Not an electric one.'

Connie reached across for the ashtray. For a moment Jane smelt the light, flowery perfume Connie always used — it echoed persuasively in her clothes, in her bedroom, in rooms she visited; it was a part of Connie, and Jane, who had never smelt it on any one else, had secretly hung her nose over perfume testers in chemists all over the place but had never been able to track it down. It reminded her of summer. For some reason she felt silly, shy of asking Connie its name.

'You don't go out much,' she accused her. 'You must get fed up staying in. I know *I* would.'

'I don't think about it.'

'Staying in makes one dull.'

Connie, with a little smile, said: 'Well, I have so much to do.' She looked sideways at Daniel. 'I mean by the time I've got the children to bed and David's nappies soaked and we've had dinner and I've washed up and scrubbed the sink and cut the grapefruits ready for breakfast, I don't feel like going out.' In spite of her tone, the little smile was still there.

Jane, unaware that she was being teased, said: 'You lay breakfast the night before? Sounds like a boarding house.'

Connie almost laughed. 'Well, I have to,' she managed to say, 'or I'd never get the children's handkerchiefs ironed for school and Daniel's—' she nudged him under the table '—overcoat brushed properly.'

'Poor thing! Everyone thinks you're awfully domesticated—I mean, homely—but I never realised you thought like this about it. I'll show you some short cuts. And we could do an evening class together once or twice a week. What about squash?'

Daniel's mouth twitched, and Connie, who was shaking with the effort not to laugh, stared hard at the table. Then she thought of her house, of sitting by the fire, and she could see no reason why she should ever leave it.

The head waiter padded over and gave his panda's smile. Behind his back his hand made signals, and a tray of sweets was brought to the table. 'On the house, sir. And would you like me to keep this table for Wednesday, sir? Or would you rather have the corner?'

'I'm not certain it will be Wednesday. It depends when my clients arrive.'

'I'll keep the table for an hour, sir?'

Daniel said decisively. 'Yes, keep it. My secretary will cancel

11

if necessary. Friday week I'd like a table for six.'

'Very good, Mr Stein. Very good, sir.'

'I'm handling the Bryant case. The old man's flying over from the States. We're in court ten days,' he told Mark.

'How will it go?' asked Mark.

'Oh, we'll win,' he said lightly.

'You must hate it when Daniel's out in the evenings,' said Jane.

'Usually he's only out when he's doing the free advice evenings, but now because of the flat project and—'

'You must hate it.'

'I don't mind being on my own. I quite like it.'

'If your husband's a Labour councillor, you can forget your cosy evenings round the fire talking about squash,' said Daniel. 'A Conservative councillor—well that's another thing.' He winked at Mark.

'Get an au pair,' said Jane.

'Don't want one,' said Connie.

'You'd be much freer,' said Jane ferociously.

'Where you read rights for the Left, I read houses for the middle-class at lower cost. Why should—'

Jane snorted, and the sound terrified a man at the next table. 'Enough of this,' she said, getting up. 'You can discuss all this any time. Come on.' She took Connie's arm. 'We've got a special birthday surprise.'

3

Jane's surprise was a crowded nightclub in the West End, and they sat near the floorshow watching six girls, dressed as tigers, slither through a jungle number. Their breasts were bare, their eyes bored. Any interest they might have unearthed in Mark was quelled immediately by the music, which was so loud he had to cover his ears. Jane alone managed to shout above it. 'This isn't the surprise.' The music got louder, the girls spun faster, the lights cut out—Mark looked as though he'd have to be carried out. During the polite applause a spotlight picked out the Master of Ceremonies as he swished on to the floor.

'And now what we've all been waiting for. He's taken them by storm in Paris, thrilled them in Berlin, and now, on his first-ever visit to London, we have the exclusive pleasure of bringing to you, the Magician from Hungary, the Greatest Magician in the World, Danchenko!'

Jane cried: 'He's supposed to be terrific.'

The lights changed colour several times as he came on in a cloud of white doves, produced a doubtful rabbit from a black hat and juggled a hoop, a ball and a skittle successfully. A pink chiffon scarf gave birth to multicoloured chiffon scarves.

'It's not feasible to have the bloody thing spread all over London,' said Daniel. 'What d'you want? A fleet of taxis to take patients from haemotology to X-ray?'

'I just said it spoils the view,' murmured Mark.

Drums rolled, doves disappeared, the magician climbed on to a small dais, and Mark fell asleep.

'He used to be a councillor before he became articulate—'

'Wake up, Mark!' Jane hissed. She passed him his drink.

'I'm not asleep, for Godsake.'

The magician was thin, dramatic; and he could have been any age. The MC stretched up and blindfolded him with three thick scarves.

'. . . No. I've never actually heard Lewis talk,' said Daniel. 'He grunts. When he belches they mistake it for a protest and call point of order. Jenkins is the only tricky one. But I'll push it through.'

'Not once, not twice, but three times for Danchenko! Now I will touch any object you choose and Danchenko will identify it.' The MC moved swiftly among the tables with his black tails whipping from side to side — he looked like a snake. 'What am I touching now, Maestro?'

'Now you have a handkerchief. It is a woman's handkerchief. Not new. Into it has flowed many tears, but the handkerchief will now stay dry. The cause of the tears is over.'

'You'll have a free hand, Mark.'

'I've got a lot on.'

'You'll do it,' said Jane happily. 'You'll fit it in. I want to get out of Europe this summer.'

'What am I touching?'

'A glass.'

'And now?'

'Another glass.'

Laughter. 'You can't fool Danchenko,' said the MC.

'Come out to the lavatory, Mark, and I'll give you a dozen reasons why you should.'

Jane, waving her watch, jumped up and down, among the crowd all vying for attention. The MC, dismayed by her flapping hair and digging fingers, had no choice, and the watch was forced into his hand. He just stopped her holding up his arm by doing it himself.

'Now, Danchenko.'

'A wristwatch with a thin strap. I feel it is too tight.'

Jane's mouth hung open.

'The wearer of this watch has a strong wrist. The pulse is often very fast but strong. The person does much running. The arm sometimes waves strenuously, but not goodbye to a lover she no longer has use for, nor again to warn a lover she likes that her husband is home.' Laughter. 'She is playing tennis.' Loud applause and the MC escaped over to the other side of the room.

'I can't Wednesday,' said Daniel. 'The Lord Mayor's having a thing at the Goldsmith's Hall. Have a stab at the drawings and—'

'Did you hear that?' asked Jane.

'Terrific,' said Daniel.

'And what am I holding here, Maestro?'

'You are touching a bald head.'

Laughter.

'It's all done by code,' Daniel told Jane. 'Or he can see.'

'Well, he couldn't see my strap was too tight. Still, it's not the only thing tight around here. Wake up, Mark. Pull yourself together.'

'A glass,' said Danchenko.

'What's in the glass?' shouted a man in the audience.

'Give him something of yours, Daniel. Give him—' Jane looked at his coat, then at Connie. 'Give him her brooch. Go on, Dan.'

He stiffened. He'd made rather a point of always being called Daniel.

'Amber liquid. It wont be there long.' Men around the table cheered. The magician leaned forward. Suddenly his blindfold eyes seemed to peer into the audience. In a low menacing voice, he said: 'The glass forever emptying, forever refilling. A sorrow is being swilled away. A hardening liver can be more sorrowful, my friend. Take an old magic man's advice.'

During the shocked silence, Daniel was heard to say, 'Isn't there a bar or something? Let's go and discuss it properly. The girls are all right. They're having fun.'

'Too near the mark, Maestro,' someone bellowed.

The magician chuckled.

'His laugh isn't the funniest thing in the world,' said Jane. She looked at Daniel—at his mouth, firm and decisive, at his yellow eyes, penetrating, steady—and she looked so hard she nearly missed the next bit and Connie nudged her. The MC was holding his hand up in the air.

'And now?'

'Do not think you are touching nothing, my friend. The air is not empty but full of vibrations.'

Daniel held out Connie's brooch, but the MC, attracted to a nail-file at the next table, turned his back and was about to reach for it, when Jane, grabbing the brooch, swung it like lightning in front of the almost victorious nail-file and dumped

15

it unceremoniously on to the MC's outstretched hand. She'd won too many relay races to let her side be ignored, and the MC, startled by her, was obliged to hold it up and say: 'And now?'

The magician shuddered. Perhaps it was his black, flowing clothes that made the action so terrifying. Conversation died, forgotten. Jane still tipped the champagne bottle against her glass. All around were objects, held out, held up, dangling, foolish. Only the cigarette smoke carried on drifting up, unafraid.

'A heart,' and he smiled — a long cavernous smile that made his face look like a Halloween lantern. Then the audience started to move, to mutter. A man at the next table leaned across to Jane. The MC, disconcerted, tried to hand the brooch back. The noise grew, and through it the magician said quietly: 'A heart. It will not be gashed or cut or crushed but taken whole and still beating from the body.'

Stunned, Connie turned to Daniel. He was talking to Mark. No longer believing what she'd heard, she said, 'Did you hear that?'

'What?' asked Mark.

She grabbed Jane. 'Did you hear it?' Then she saw a woman at the next table looking at her. She'd heard it. She was appalled.

'He said something about a heart,' said Jane.

'"It will not be cut or . . .".' He said that,' said Connie. Jane looked at her, startled.

'I didn't hear that. Come on, Maestro. It's her birthday,' she shouted.

The magician had taken his blindfold off and the MC was gliding on to the floor. The drums rolled, people clapped; but the atmosphere in the club was not as festive as it had been.

The magician walked slowly forward and pointed a long finger at a man at the back. 'Bring me that glass, my friend.'

Amid a few calls and whistles ('Watch it or he'll turn you into a rabbit'), the man went self-consciously up to Danchenko and gave him the glass.

Danchenko said softly: 'What the magician touches brings luck. And now a small thing.' He peered into the audience, and here and there an object was held out to him. 'An

16

ear-ring? No, not an ear-ring.' He bent towards a middle-aged fat woman and chuckled. 'Beware your ear hears too much gossip. A cackling woman and a crowing hen bring no luck to cock or hen.'

'He's got that wrong,' murmured Jane. She was staring at Daniel again. 'Hasn't he?' She squirmed long and luxuriously. It seemed to relieve something. He looked away.

The magician's black-rimmed eyes swung over the room, searching. They flicked on to Connie, and flicked away; but it was she he chose. The long finger pointed unquestionably at her. 'And now bring me the heart.'

'Go on,' said Jane, excited.

'How did he know who it belonged to?' asked Daniel.

'He must have seen Jane give it back,' said Mark.

Connie got up and walked on to the centre of the floor, her soft dark hair blue in the strange light. The magician held the heart for a moment, and then said, 'A clean cut of the knife. Beware the reformer.'

Connie stared at him. Then she turned and went back to her place. She was still moving gracefully.

The magician did a complicated trick, during which he turned red, and then green. There was smoke, the doves flew round, the glass and the heart disappeared, and Connie thought, 'How did he know the brooch was mine?'

As though encouraged by the half light, Jane's leg shifted so close to Daniel it must almost have been touching him.

Daniel was looking at Mark. 'Will you do it?'

It was after four as they walked along a deserted road to the car. Daniel, though short-legged and pudgy, moved with surprising agility and had more speed even than Jane.

'The baby-sitter had better stay the night — what's left of it,' said Connie. 'It was fun, but I didn't like his laugh.'

'He's a fake,' said Daniel.

'He is not, Dan!' Jane pranced up and down like a horse.

Seeing her husband's expression, Connie said, '*Daniel* doesn't believe in the supernatural.'

'When will you get the drawings in?' Daniel asked Mark.

'End of the week,' said Jane. 'He got my watch strap being tight.'

'Law of averages,' said Daniel. 'He certainly isn't Hungarian.'

'What are you muttering about?' Jane asked Mark. 'Yes, you'll have time. I'll let you off the hour with the kid each night and you'll have a clear run. Poor old Connie. Beating hearts and beware informers.'

'*Re*formers,' said Mark.

'Hardly a birthday greeting,' she said. 'Anyway, how do you know? You were asleep most of the time. At least Dan doesn't fall asleep.' Her voice was slurred.

'Yes, what was all that about?' asked Mark. 'I thought I heard him say something about cutting things out from a body.'

'I didn't hear that,' said Daniel. 'I'm sure he didn't say that.'

'He did,' said Connie. 'Everyone was making such a noise. I wonder what it means.'

'Nothing to worry about,' said Jane. 'Probably an abortion.'

Connie shuddered.

'And what about your departing and approaching lovers?' said Daniel.

'Huh!' Jane flushed. She had, unknown to the men, but known to Connie, just trifled with a lean young tennis player. 'I wonder where we'll go on Connie's next birthday.'

Connie was aware of the street without looking at it. It was narrow, ordinary, its buildings vague, except for a lighted shop-front here and there, and at the end Regent's Street brimming with light. Suddenly it all changed. The lights didn't look right. The corner of the street moved, and the tailor's shop was something else. She stopped, and blinked; but when she opened her eyes the street was all right again.

'Forgotten something?' Daniel asked.

'Too much to drink.'

4

Connie's kitchen was large, and its long harsh lights made the red-and-black tiled floor jump and dazzle, with all the impact of a migraine attack. The rugs were away at the cleaners. When they were there the kitchen was cosy. Old, useless things on their various journeys from other parts of the house to the dustcart had congregated there and stayed. There was a dilapidated rocking-chair that squealed if touched, an ancient mangle with nonsensical legs, an enormous radiogram, its insides long since gone; and these things, like aged and stubborn relatives, had their place and refused to move or be humiliated by the rest of the kitchen, which gleamed and was impeccably the latest thing.

Connie, dressed in long striped socks, slippers and a short skirt, was sweeping the floor. Her green-and-white striped sweater emphasised her body and the hazel-green of her eyes. She bent to pick up a crust and saw, beneath the table, other things that had a way of gathering there—the forbidden toys.

'Daniel!' she shouted. 'Tell the horrors to come down and take their stuff up to the playroom. I keep telling them.' She waited optimistically for a reply, and then, when there wasn't one, went to the door and shouted, 'Right! I'm throwing them out.'

'Coming, Mum,' called the child least likely to come.

Daniel wasn't fooled and shouted from his study, 'Adam! Do what your mother tells you.'

Connie shoved her mending-basket and the heap of clothes to be ironed further along the wooden table and wiped the new space with kitchen paper. She fetched a plate piled with raw meat from the fridge; and as she did so Daniel came in and put down his coffee cup, a screwdriver, a door-handle, and the space was gone. 'I'll propose Mark for the new scheme if I can get it through.' The heap of ironing overflowed on to the floor. 'We're voting tonight.'

Connie kicked the fridge-door shut and hurried across with the heavy plate. 'Move all that,' she said, eyeing the screwdriver.

'I want to talk to him. He'd be good, you know. But I must do it somewhere where she can't possibly be, or he'll never get a word in.'

'Male sauna,' and she pushed the plate to the end of the table and got a chopping board from the drawer.

The overhead light started whirring, and like an answering mating call the pipes started rattling. At the other side of the kitchen the fridge did its bobbing-and-shaking dance.

'Pub,' he said. 'Tomorrow lunchtime.'

'But he doesn't want to do it.'

'We'll go round the corner to the Crown. Lamb's Conduit Street's too crowded.'

Connie found a recipe book and put on her big shiny apron. The fridge slowed down, and there was sudden silence.

Daniel pressed himself against her back and stroked her breast. 'He gets quite soppy about the changing face of London. I don't know it he's got illusions or just rather commonplace scruples.'

'He's sensitive.'

'He'll grow out of it.' He left her breast alone and ate a hunk of cheese. 'She's not always as bad as the other night. She seems to get louder when she's with you, for some reason. He's quite worn out by her. No wonder people think he's dull.'

'She's a good friend, Daniel. Her heart's in the right place.'

She went over to the other side of the kitchen, over to the long sink unit with its jangling jungle of metal implements, tricks and time-savers, and picked out her sharpest knife.

Daniel checked his watch with the electric clock. 'Yes, I'll get him to the pub.'

'I wish you'd get them to take their stuff upstairs. I wait on them hand and foot.'

'I've told you. You've devalued a mother's best weapon. No television.'

'Threats are no good. I—'

'Of course they're no good,' he shouted. 'You never carry them out. Just take the plug out.' He ate a tomato and looked at the collection Connie had put by the door. 'The sight of

20

Dolly Deirdre in the dustbin now . . .'

In the twitching strip-lighting, Connie's face was flawless, serene. Its only signs of age were small lines at the corners of her eyes—upward, optimistic lines. Her eyes, beautiful in shape and colour, had a rare combination of elusiveness and good humour. Her eyes were all you really noticed, some people said; and that was lucky, they added, because her looks were so ordinary.

'It would really be one up, you know, if I could get Mark to do it.'

Upstairs the battle of the television channels raged, and the losers gave the action a last twist by screeching. It brought Daniel up there in a flash and the plug was pulled out.

Connie cut the meat.

'Adam's getting smug,' said Daniel coming back. 'The answer is two television sets, Dad,' he mimicked. 'Why should I watch crap?'

She smiled and shifted the cut-off fat to one side.

'What's it going to be?' he asked, looking over her shoulder.

'Steak and kidney pie.'

'Plenty of crust.'

'Jane says you're getting horribly fat.' She went on cutting.

'Has he done his homework, by the way?' he asked, and rushed out.

The meat was tough suddenly.

Upstairs, her eldest son discovered that his father's idea of hard work did not match his.

The meat became fleshy, knotty. It seeped bloodily. She cut again, and blood spurted out, ran over her hands, spread blackly over the chopping board. She put the knife down carefully and backed away, trying to wipe her hands on the slippery apron. Then the meat looked all right again. She stared at it. The blood seemed less. She turned and walked slowly across the kitchen. The red polished floor was blinding.

Daniel was in the living-room putting papers in his briefcase.

'Darling, would you cut the meat for me?'

He looked up, surprised. 'But I'm just off. Use a sharper knife. You all right?'

She nodded.

21

'You look quite pale.' He kissed her quickly and hurried to the front door. 'Ring Jane, will you, and go on to her about exotic holidays. Three weeks in India. No, that's too cheap. Safari. That's it. She'd enjoy that. Back about midnight — if Jenkins doesn't stir the idiots up too much.'

When he'd gone, she crept back into the kitchen. Upstairs, children splashed in the bath. Timidly, she approached the meat. It looked like stewing steak. She started cutting again.

It was curious, that change in the meat, she thought. For a moment it had looked alive.

5

It was almost dark as Jane and Connie, both carrying Sainsbury bags piled high with food, stood on the corner of Willoughby Road near the heath.

'I'm fed up with Mark,' said Jane, putting down her carrier. 'He shuts himself up in his room and works every evening. What life do I get? I'm sure he doesn't have to work so much. The kid and me are important as well. You must get fed up with Daniel being out so much.'

'Well, I'd rather he was home, but there's a lot happening on the council at the moment. Have you talked to Mark about it?'

'Of course. He just retreats even further. And now Daniel's waving this new project under his nose. I don't know what to think. I don't know whether we should do it or not. I'd like the money.' She hopped from foot to foot and banged her big fur mittens together. 'Anyway I'm off with you-know-who tonight, I'll say I'm with you, so please back me up.'

Connie hesitated, and then said reluctantly: 'Well, all right. What if he rings?'

'He won't. Haven't you ever wanted a change?'

'Well, I suppose there've been men I've thought attractive, yes, but it's never gone further than that. I suppose its because I'm O.K. with Daniel.'

'You still feel the same about each other sexually after ten years? I don't believe it.'

'No, it's not the same. It's better, if anything. But it goes in cycles. Sometimes for days we hardly notice each other.'

'You're lucky.' Jane was envious but open about it. 'Still, Daniel's put on weight. I told him so. Doesn't he do any sports? I thought he said he was good at athletics.'

'He doesn't have time.'

'His eyes really look at you, don't they? That's what makes

him attractive. Mark goes round as though he's blanketed in thick fog. Still, I must be off, if I'm going to — you know.'

'Jane, have you ever had something happen to you where things you're looking at change shape . . . texture . . . just for a moment?'

Jane laughed. 'Frequently — if I've drunk a bit too much.'

'I'm serious.'

'Then, no.'

'I can't tell if it's the things or my perceptions. It's happened the past few days.'

'Tiredness. Eyestrain. Anyway, I must go.'

Connie walked home. The dark streets seemed too empty. There were people about — a long way off. The wind blew the trees and she heard footsteps behind her, a man's footsteps, getting nearer. Nervously she walked faster, but the other person was catching up. When he was almost up to her she gasped, and swiftly crossed the road. The man gave her a quick, surprised look and carried on walking. At the end of the road he went into his house, and Connie, her heart still thumping, felt rather silly.

The next day Connie was sprawled in the huge padded chair, watching television. Her eyes were half-closed and she looked fluffy and full of curves like a big cat. A book lay open at her feet, and beside her the electric fire, full on, sent its never-dying flames leaping up the tin grate; the coals twinkled rhythmically. The curtains weren't drawn. Outside, the trees, taller than anything around them, stretched up into the clear night sky. A breeze flapped around them. They creaked and the smaller branches jabbed against the roof.

The programme faded, and on came the adverts, blaring and bold, tumbling over each other like bad clowns. Connie stretched luxuriously, and then lay back again. She'd endure the adverts — anything rather than move.

The programme began again, but her eyes suddenly flicked over to the window. Seeing only trees they returned, rather carefully, to the television. Then she jerked up and listened. There should be a sound. She looked at the round polished table, at the hi-fi, at all the familiar things in her living room, but they didn't seem familiar any more. The trees stiffened,

24

alert, waiting, and high up a stronger breeze prowled through their branches. What was the sound she expected to hear? The television audience laughed. She sprang out of the chair and turned round. The front door, she could see, was closed. She switched off the set and, after the loud audience laughter, the house was too quiet. She didn't like the trees, the way their hard silent trunks filled the window, so she drew the curtains and stood still, scarcely breathing. There was a sharp noise in the kitchen — but it was just the fridge getting ready for its next dance. Things around her only looked recognisable when she examined each one and murmured its name. Sweating slightly and out of breath, her heart tumbling inside her, she forced herself back into the plump black chair. She turned down the fire, and the flames were obliged to twitch over coals reduced to a mere glow. She picked up the book and opened it, and put her slippers on. Her mouth was dry. She looked at the page. She looked at the clock, then at her watch. She looked into space. She looked at the clock again.

From the window, the garden seemed too long. She couldn't see the road, she realised, because the shrubs were too high. The swing didn't look harmless. The little stubbly plants she liked had disappeared. She let go the curtain. She sighed: breathing wasn't easy.

She'd go to the kitchen and make some tea. Purposefully she crossed the living room but stopped at the edge of the hallway. The staircase looked menacing. For the first time, her own house frightened her. The front door, bristling with old locks and bolts, disused and rusty, gave no security. The panels of frosted glass seemed particularly frail. She put the chain on quickly, and then remembered the back door and sped down to the kitchen to make sure it was locked.

Everything was too bright here. Alone on the dazzling floor she was exposed. She hurried back to the shadows and the dubious security of the hallway, and for some time she stood, her back pressed to the wall, alert, listening for the sound she wanted. She could almost hear it now. Then she remembered Daniel. Weak with relief, she reached across for the phone and dialled his number.

'Hello darling.' Her voice sounded too loud. 'I wondered how you're getting on.'

'All right, Catkin. Is it anything special?'

'I wondered when you were coming back.'

'I told you. I'm not sure. Are you all right?'

'I'm feeling a bit shaky.'

'Maybe you're getting flu.'

'I'm worried about that chain.'

'What chain?'

'The chain on the bloody door.'

'Connie!'

'It's all right. It's all right. But the kitchen locks aren't any good. They're rusty. Any—'

'Connie. I've got to go back to the meeting. I'm holding everyone up. Look, you sound as though you're getting a touch of something. Have a scotch, a strong one, and go to bed.' He hung up.

She poured (she was not an accustomed drinker) what she considered a strong one. It tasted vile. She went upstairs and looked at her sleeping children. Listening to them breathe made her feel better.

Coming down the stairs she saw something—something on the wall, on the curving wall of the stairway. It was a huge shadow of a man. Terrified, she turned round. There was only the stairs and the boxes on the landing. She looked at the shadow. It *looked* like a man and his arm was raised high above his head. She'd never seen the shadow before.

She walked down to the phone, her legs tingling and stiff, and as her shadow passed into the other it looked as though the arm was about to strike her.

She called Jane.

'So you've heard the news?' Jane said immediately.

'No Jane. Look I'm—'

'Daniel's proposed him for the scheme, and—'

'Look Jane. I'm feeling a bit wobbly. I don't know what it is. I've got a feeling that—'

'Yes?'

'—that someone's trying to get in.'

Jane gave an animal shriek. 'Let's hope it's someone nice.'

'Jane,' she said hesitantly. 'Could you come round?'

'Oh Connie. I can't. There's no one with the kid. Mark's out. Go to a neighbour.'

'They're a long way away.'

'Don't be ridiculous.'

'Well, they seem a long way. I've got to go down that long garden and through the gate—'

'Hop over a wall.'

Connie, hurt, didn't say anything. Jane said, 'No really. Go over the wall. It doesn't sound like you.'

'I've been feeling a bit odd for days.'

'Pregnant. You're pregnant again. You know that awful early stage.'

Connie sat down, dazed with relief. 'That's it. That's why the meat looked funny.'

'Get yourself a big drink and watch television. Get your mind off it. We'll see you Thursday. So long kid.'

Then she heard the sound she had been expecting. It seemed to come from a long long way away. It was the sound of heavy, wooden wheels and a child's squeaky voice shouting, '*Watercresses!*'

Something woke her. She lay, not breathing, wondering what the noise had been. Without turning in the bed, she knew she was alone. A muffled noise downstairs coming from the hallway, the noise of someone trying to get in. She jolted up. 'Cor.' The expression lingered in her mind, even after she heard Daniel's voice call, 'Connie, open the door.'

She was so relieved, she half fell on the stairs in the rush to get to him. The door jammed; she'd forgotten the chain. Dithering, she took it off and clung to him and 'Cor!' clung to her mind and she couldn't get rid of it.

'All right, Catkin.' He comforted her. 'What's happened?'

She shook her head.

He sat her gently on the stairs. 'Why did you have the chain on?'

She looked at him, at his dark eyes, at his black sleek hair, at his pallor, at his firm mouth, at all those things she loved. Then she remembered the shadow.

Without looking, she pointed above her head, upwards at the curving landing.

He stiffened.

'The shadow,' she whispered.

27

He frowned at her, and then darting up the stairs. 'Shadow? Shadow? What shadow?' He was tired, on edge. She came up behind him.

'There,' and she pointed at the thick, looming shape.

He looked at it as though he was in an art gallery viewing pictures way beyond his comprehension. He frowned, blinked, bent sideways. 'It's always been there, Connie,' was all he could find to say about it.

'It hasn't.'

'For Godsake!'

'I haven't seen it.' She was nearly crying.

'Anyway, what about it?'

'Ssh!' indicating the children. 'Can't you see?' she whispered. He turned and looked at her.

'It's — it's a man isn't it?' she said.

'No Connie, it isn't a man. It's a meaningless shape caused by the landing.' He turned and looked upwards, searching.

'But he's holding his arm up. Can't you see that?'

'That's a box. That long box up there. Jutting out.' He ran up four stairs, pushed the box up so it rested against the wall and the menacing arm disappeared. 'It must have fallen down.'

'Oh,' she murmured. 'I am sorry.' The shadow was now nothing more than a big blob.

'It must have fallen yesterday when I was getting my old case notes out,' he explained patiently. 'It stuck out and caused that shape. It's five to one. Now let's get some sleep. Please.'

The next night she sat in the kitchen sewing her daughter's dress. The electric clock thumped out the minutes and a chicken soup bubbled on the stove. It was full of home-grown herbs and smelt delicious. Connie bit through the thread, put the dress gently on the table and went up to the curving stairway. She looked at the shadow. It was exactly as it had been before he moved the box. A man loomed up, his arm raised and somehow she knew, before she even turned, that the long box would be up against the wall and not jutting out.

6

On Thursday evening they sat at the oval table in Connie's small dining room. There were long white candles, white roses, a crisp white table cloth. They'd just enjoyed, or said they had, Connie's first attempt at home-made cannellonis in Neapolitan sauce. The frozen beans had been excellent. The dinner was to celebrate Mark getting the Camden Town flat project and there were three bottles of claret on the sideboard.

Connie was wearing the scarlet velvet dress Daniel had bought for her birthday, and her shoulder-length hair was pinned up in a chignon. She didn't wear the diamond brooch and nobody mentioned it. Jane, who again wore her prim black frock, said she was impressed with the way Connie looked and she kept nudging Mark. 'Doesn't she look old-fashioned?'

Exhaustion had already got a foothold on his evening and he sighed 'Yes. Yes.' His wife was getting loud again, but at least it wasn't in public.

'Everyone should have a deep freeze,' said Jane.

'Nonsense,' Mark replied, his voice high and cracking. 'They're just a fad. You've survived all this time without one.'

'That's no reason for not having one. I want one. Why shouldn't I have one?' Her eyes gleamed maliciously. 'You have what you want. What about that 12-function calculator you got last month? You can work perfectly well without it but I didn't stop you having it.'

'It seems amazing people ever got by without refrigerators,' said Daniel and scooped up the last beans.

'Think,' said Jane, looking at his fleshy chin and the suggestion of others under it.

He grinned and cut a huge lump of bread.

She poked her tongue out and then turned to Connie. 'I'm saving up for a deep freeze. I don't know whether to get a really big one, like you've got, or an upright one.'

Mark gave her a baleful glance. 'There's no room.'

'There will be, Mark. There will be,' and her staccato laugh made him fear for his 12-function calculator and all his other luxuries.

'I'm thinking of placing the flats round a central space area.' Mark said, rather awkwardly.

'How will you fill the space?' asked Daniel.

'I wasn't thinking of filling it.'

'Christine across the road from me has just got a washing-up machine,' said Jane. 'It's the only thing for that job.'

'Only for large families,' said Daniel.

'Rubbish! For any family. Why not? Though why she needs one, when she's got an au pair, I don't know.'

'I was thinking of having just grass,' said Mark.

Daniel shrugged and looked at the sideboard. 'You'll have trouble getting grass past Jenkins. He wants a shopping precinct included in the scheme.'

'But there's shops all round —'

'A modern shopping precinct, split-level. Where's the chocolate, Connie?'

'You know Christine. Her husband's in advertising. She wears loads of make-up even first thing in the morning. Mark's seen her before seven with eyelashes on.'

Connie's youngest boy David came running into the room, a baby's bottle hanging by its teat from between his teeth.

'Go to bed, angel,' Connie said softly.

'Want lilly juice.'

'Bed!' roared Daniel and the child tottered off.

'What's lilly juice?' asked Jane.

'Gripe water.' Connie laughed. 'He'll never grow up.'

'The kid's the same about —'

'Would you support me?' Mark asked suddenly. 'I mean — what do *you* think?'

'Sure,' Daniel said rather absently.

'You see, it would be a play area. I'll show you the new drawings.'

'The drawings should be simple. Straight up and down.'

'No, there's no problem about —'

'Pass your glass, Jane, Connie. Try this one — . . .'

'It's not twenty pound a night,' said Mark.

The candles had gone right down, and wax dripped over the holders and hung suspended in obscene, horrid shapes. Connie stared at them.

'It is,' Jane insisted.

'On the *wagon-lit*, she means,' said Daniel; and he opened another bottle.

Connie was leaning, elbow on the table, head resting in her hand, precariously. Her eyes were unseeing and the exact purpose of the evening was no longer clear.

'For two,' said Mark.

'Twenty pound a night,' shouted Jane.

Connie heard, quite clearly, another voice say, *'It's fourpence a night for the doss house, Liz. Otherwise it's the casual ward.'*

'It's ten pound each, stupid,' said Jane.

The other, a rough, deep Cockney voice, said, *'If you go in the casual ward you've got to stay there two days.'*

'You don't want to try Flower and Dean Street?' Connie said and her head lurched off her hand. She jerked it up again.

'What?' asked Daniel.

'In Buck Row it's mixed. You can sleep two to a bed,' and Connie giggled.

They all stared at her. 'Are you all right?' Jane asked.

Connie, suddenly bewildered, tried to laugh. 'Of course I'm all right.'

'Well, what's all this two-to-a-bed?' asked Jane.

Connie tried to laugh again. 'Just a joke.' She poured some wine and her fork fell on the floor. A vague sense of her position as hostess came back to her and she said to Mark, in a loud voice, 'Congratulations!'

They were staring at her. Then Jane said firmly, 'It's a hell of a price for one night,' and drew the men's attention off Connie. 'I'd rather sit up. Wouldn't you? Except of course if you've got the kids with you. Then no price would be too high.'

'The other night she put the chain on the door,' Daniel told Mark, quietly.

'Well, that's not such a bad idea,' he murmured.

'No. That's not what I mean.'

'I don't even sleep in a *wagon lit*,' said Jane. 'It's either too

31

hot or too cold. It's always noisy.'

'We've lived here for over ten years,' said Daniel. She loves this house. It was my mother's house.'

Connie gulped her wine and poured some more. Her way of drinking became unfamiliar. It was out of control, angular.

'Half the time the back door isn't locked even when she goes out,' Daniel said. 'We've got nothing to steal after all.' He looked at Connie, who was swaying a bit, and winced.

'It may be her nerves,' muttered Mark. That was a complaint he was familiar with.

Jane pounced on 'nerves'. She knew all about 'nerves'. 'It is not her nerves. Anyone can see she's pregnant.'

The men looked at Jane, astounded. She'd got their attention and she meant to keep it. 'Women go through funny changes at the beginning of pregnancies.'

'But she's not been like this before,' Daniel said, timidly.

'Every pregnancy is different, Daniel. She'll be all right after the 12th week. Anyway, she wanted another one.'

Connie was poised between the desire to pour her next drink and oblivion. She stroked her thigh in an inviting way, then looked down sharply.

'What have you dropped?' asked Jane.

'I touched my dress. It felt rough. Then I look down. I see velvet.' She hiccoughed.

'They're lovely flowers,' said Jane brightly.

'Daniel got them for me. He gets me such lovely presents.' She emphasised the 'lovely' and giggled.

Daniel clapped a hand over her glass. 'That's enough.'

'I wish Mark would,' said Jane. 'Get presents I mean.' She hooted with laughter.

Connie started singing, at first hesitantly.

> 'Oh, they say I killed a man, so they said.
> Oh, they say I killed a man, so they said.
> For I hit him on the 'ead
> With a bloody great lump of lead
> Damn 'is eyes.
> Oh they put me—'

'Shut up!' said Daniel.

Jane took her arm. 'What about a bit of air? Come on.'

Connie wouldn't move. There was a different expression on her face. She looked—lewd. 'Pass the bottle, love,' she said to Mark.

'Time to go,' said Mark, waving his eyebrows at Jane. 'We'll walk back. It's a fresh night.'

Connie bawled,

> 'Oh they put me into quod
> All for killing of that sod.'

Daniel, aghast, said, 'Shut up!'

> 'They did so 'elp me Gawd
> Damn their eyes.'

Embarrassed, Jane tried to join in, but she didn't know the words.

Connie slumped on to the table, knocking her glass over.

'She did want another one,' Jane said again.

Connie murmured. 'Another new bonnet, pretty one. It cost a sovereign. That's not a bloody sovereign, you bugger. It's a church farthing. You polished it up.'

Mark, hoping to save Daniel further embarrassment, got their coats and waited in the hallway. Daniel opened the front door.

'Just have a pee,' and Jane ran upstairs.

Mark hesitated, and then said, 'Could I see you before the planning permission meeting? I'd like to get the idea across to—'

Daniel shook his head abruptly. 'I doubt if I'll make the meeting. I've got the Bryant case all this week and I'm eager to get that derelict area near Lisson Grove used properly. They're talking about building some damn silly composition football pitch.'

Connie started singing again.

'She's got quite a voice,' said Jane, adjusting her dress.

Daniel almost shoved them out and then hurried back to the dining room.

'Come on. Bed!'

'Why should I go with you?' She waved a finger at him. 'You've got me mixed up.'

Connie lay dizzily in bed, a cold flannel on her forehead, a glass of Alka Seltzer fizzing murderously beside her. She was talking into the phone, and every word had to be dragged up with great effort. David ran round and round the room.

'I'm sorry about last night, Jane. Was I awful?'

'Pretty drunk.'

'I can't remember a thing. Daniel's furious. I spilt wine all over the cloth. He had to do everything—this morning. I couldn't move.'

'Have you been sick?'

'Not yet. Anyway, say sorry to Mark. It's not something I'll do again, believe me.'

'I wouldn't. You're just not yourself when you're like that. It's like being with a different person.'

7

Spring was early and Connie moved David's toys on to the lawn and started preparing her flower borders and vegetable patch. She hadn't seen Jane for some days and she arrived unexpectedly as Connie was running round the garden with David.

'How've you been?' Jane asked.

'Fine.'

They sat on the grass.

'It's such a good day I thought I'd go on the heath.'

'I hope it doesn't go cold again. It'll kill everything.'

'I've just had another set-to with Mark. I want a deep freeze and a hi-fi. He says we can only have a deep freeze. He's astonishing. He's not really mean, just careful, and there's no reason for it, especially now he's got the new thing from Daniel. You must come to dinner with us. Daniel's amazing the speed he gets things done.' After a pause she asked, 'Done any more take-offs of the Good Old Days lately?'

Connie shivered.

'I know Daniel didn't go much on the coarse bits, but Mark was terribly impressed. I mean, you knew it all through. Where did you learn it?'

'I don't know,' she said quietly.

'You couldn't have heard it at boarding school — though on the other hand boarding school is probably just the place you would.'

'That must be it.'

'What would you do about the hi-fi? I feel like just going and getting one.'

'Well, do.' Connie was preoccupied.

'Don't you and Daniel ever have rows?'

She shook her head without thinking.

'You don't belong in Hampstead. With a marriage like yours you ought to be living in Golders Green.'

Connie, wearing her latest dress, yellow, short and backless, stood at the sink. The sound of voices talking and shouting, police whistles, and feet running, started up among the clatter of plates and noise of running water.

'No one came out of Buck's Row.'

'Some sneaky yid who wouldn't pay for his fun.'

'She cut up nasty.'

'Come quickly for gawd's sake. It's something horrible.'

She turned off the tap and, almost collapsing, held on to the sink. Around her there were only the ordinary noises of the kitchen. A plate was broken.

'Aren't you cold?' asked Daniel, suddenly behind her. 'It's a very appealing number, but I don't want strawberries and cream getting cold.' He patted her bare back. 'Back when I can, Catkin.'

'Don't go!'

'Oh Connie.'

'Please don't go. I can't stand it.'

'What, dear?'

And then she turned round and he saw her face. The fluorescent strip-light had whited out all colour from it.

'Connie!'

'Being alone. I can't stand it.'

In a responsible tone he said, 'Now look here. You were alone Sunday night and perfectly all right. I've got to do my stint at the Neighbourhood Law Centre. I can't just not go.'

'Not tonight. Please not tonight.' She started crying.

'You'll wake the children! Oh Connie, I'm sorry.' He touched her cheek. 'Come on, old girl.' He had no idea how to cope with the situation and he was badly alarmed. 'You'll be all right. You've got to do some pulling together. Now I'll only—'

She shrieked, 'Someone is trying to kill me!'

She stood, quite still, appalled at what she'd said.

'Now stop it! Stop it!' he said, anticipating a storm of hysterics. 'Stop it!'

She didn't move or speak. Slightly reassured, he pulled over a chair and sat her in it. He gave her a drink of water. When she did speak her voice was calm.

'That shadow came back and you wouldn't see it. It came

36

back even though you moved the box. I showed you but you wouldn't see.'

'The shadow didn't change,' he said.

'You said the box made that arm.'

'I moved the bloody box.'

'The arm came back. It's there now.'

Exasperated, he said, 'I'm going to phone Jane.'

Jane looked at the shadow and laughed loudly. 'It's—it's—I don't know what it is. It's like the blotting paper test they do for your personality. Everyone interprets it differently.'

'But how do you see it?' asked Daniel.

'A cloud. Oh, I don't know.' He was standing close to her, and she was suddenly embarrassed.

'Well, Jane, would you say it looked like a man with his arm raised?'

She hopped up and down, her body in a turmoil. She almost touched him. 'Yes, it could be. Yes, now you come to mention it.'

Downstairs, Connie waited, sullen.

Jane held Connie's hand as they sat in the kitchen. She'd just cooked some dinner but Connie wouldn't touch it. Jane nudged her. 'Come on. Eat up.'

The meat looked more meaty than it should. It was sinuous, knotty. Nauseated, Connie pushed the plate away.

'You're all right,' said Jane. 'I mean you've got everything.'

Then Connie heard the sound again. In the distance the child's voice cried, '*Watercresses. Four bunches a penny.*'

She looked almost slyly at Jane. Jane hadn't heard it.

'You've got a bloke who's nuts about you, a super house, good health, lovely kids that you wanted. This is no time to crack up.'

Daniel came into the kitchen.

'You're early,' said Jane brightly.

'I came back.' He took his coat off and looked at Jane, like a conspirator. Connie was staring at the pepper pot. They watched her for some time. She didn't blink.

'Eat up, love,' said Jane.

It echoed in Connie's mind. '*Eat up love or you'll never go to*

37

heaven. Along came Jack and then there were seven.'

'She won't touch meat,' said Daniel.

'Then she is pregnant.' Jane was triumphant.

'No. She isn't.' He sighed, and sat at the table and took Connie's other hand. 'I'm getting an *au pair* because I think some of this—a lot of this—is strain.'

Connie shook her head.

'It can suddenly hit you. You go for years doing the same thing day after day and one day—bang!'

Jane nodded energetically.

'It isn't that.' Her voice was toneless and depressed.

'Well, for Godsake what is it?' he shouted.

'Oh do leave me alone. It's just my nerves.' She shivered and near to tears said, 'Please leave me alone.'

Offended, he got up and went out of the kitchen.

Connie's eyes filled with tears and she lit a cigarette, her hands trembling. Jane who had never seen her like this, was astonished.

'Come on. It's not like you. What's wrong? What is it?'

'I don't know. I mean—it's voices.' She sighed deeply. 'They say things I've never heard. Everything changes, just for a moment.'

For once, Jane could think of nothing to say. She'd just realised Connie was nuts.

'I don't even smell like me.' She wiped the tears off her cheeks.

'I have a bath every day, yet sometimes I *stink*.' She emphasised the word and looked at Jane.

Jane remembered the perfume, the lovely summery perfume, and was secretly pleased. Then the moment passed, and she asked, quite kindly, 'What of?'

'Sweat. Nasty sweat. And other things. Sperm. Stale sperm.' Her voice was pale, resigned.

'What d'you do then?'

'I wash again.'

'Well, use something. A deodorant. No, not a deodorant. Something stronger. An anti-perspirant. You know, one of those you spray on. They last for hours and they've got a nice smell.' She shrieked with laughter 'Help! We sound like a TV ad.' Connie smiled. 'And shave your armpits. If you're in a nervous state your sweat does smell. So remember—shave.'

8

Baffled, his world a hurting, inexplicable mess, Daniel arranged to meet Mark in a local pub after work. Mark as usual looked tired, but not as tired as Daniel. They stood at the bar, and Mark, having turned to make sure he wouldn't be overheard—an eccentric precaution considering his small voice—mumbled, 'Is there anything else?'

'What?'

'Anything apart from being alone in the house that worries her?'

'Water.'

'Water?'

'Kids in the bath. The other night David—she was washing his hair—came up from under the water and she got a funny feeling he was drowned. She said for a moment he looked dead. Damned job calming her. She won't let them near the pond at the top of the heath. It's only two inches deep, for Godsake. She hears things. Said this morning she thinks she's possessed.'

'You don't think she could be a—schizophrenic?'

'Is persecution conflict—I mean mania—a part of schizophrenia?'

'Does she have hallucinations? That's the decisive symptom with schizophrenia.' He was dimly trying to visualise the shelf of tatty psychiatric paperbacks he'd collected a month after marrying Jane. 'Withdrawal from reality.'

'Happens to everyone at some time or other,' said Daniel. He was equally authoritative. 'Three out of four women go in the bin at least once in their lives.' He swallowed his beer quickly. 'The figures may be inaccurate, but you know what I mean.'

Mark nodded. 'Change of life.'

'For heavensake! Connie's a bit young for that.'

'No. I mean, it disturbs them.'

'First it was the doors, then the windows. I've had bars and grilles put all over the place. Damned job explaining to the kids. It takes quarter of an hour to lock up at night. Then, sod it, she get's out of bed on some pretext and checks it all. Now it's the children and water.'

'Symptoms of anxiety change.' Mark looked at the ceiling. 'You treat one thing. There's another. The cause, you see, doesn't change.'

'You're talking about an anxiety—' He paused, fumbling for the name.

'Neurosis?'

'That'll do. Neurosis. Not schizophrenia.'

'Jane says Connie's worried about smells.'

'Smells?'

'Body odours.' Shyly, Mark took a long drink and plunged into the delicate question of underarms and sperm.

'She really said that?'

'The schizophrenia possibility aside, I would have bet it was a—' A long silence, and then Mark dredged up, 'phobic illness, if it wasn't for this revulsion to the smell of semen. That's important. It indicates sexual—uh—problems.' He'd just read a thick book on sexual aberrations. He knew all about that.

'She never has had. I mean—'

'They're deep-rooted. Is her father alive?'

'Why yes. What's that got to do with it?'

'A transference—uh—state is difficult to . . . It could be a transference state.'

Daniel urgently tried to think of an equally illuminating possibility. Mark definitely had the grip on all the good ones. He was deciding between nervous breakdown and premenstrual blues when Mark said, his voice croaking with pleasure, 'Guilt.'

'Sounds more like transference to me.'

Mark looked at him out of the corner of his eye. 'Actually, I'm not that sure what transference is.'

'No. Well, I'm not absolutely certain about that one.'

'I mean I know it's what a lot of people go to an analyst for. But guilt is quite common. It causes all sorts of—traumas.'

'Yep. Yep.'

'I've got a suggestion, a tentative one. It could be suppressed nymphomania.'

'*Re*pressed nymphomania, you mean. The trouble is it could be anything. There's so many damn things they get. Care for a short?'

Meanwhile, Connie, her hair pinned up, sat in the hot scented bath-water shaving her armpits.

They came back from the pub, slightly drunk, and Mark came in for a last scotch and another look at the patient. Whatever they'd been expecting, Connie morbidly gazing at the shadow or overchecking the window locks, they were not prepared for what they did see. Connie stood in the hallway, by the telephone. She was naked, wet, and blood oozed down her left breast and spilt on to the carpet — the patch by her feet was already scarlet. For a moment it seemed to Daniel there was blood everywhere.

'Doctor,' said Mark, and leaving him to tend to the blood he rang the GP.

'The blood wouldn't stop. It wouldn't stop. There was lots of blood.' She was getting hysterical.

'What were you doing?' Daniel was frantic.

'Shaving. The water's all pink. I couldn't stop the blood.'

He put a cold flannel under her arm, wrapped her in his coat while Mark located the brandy and three glasses. By the time the GP arrived the blood had stopped, but she was shaking violently and unable to speak.

The GP was puzzled. Although the cut was fairly deep, it wasn't serious enough to cause such shock. He gave her two injections, one for tetanus, helped her to swallow a glucose drink, disinfected the cut and covered it with gauze. Then he took Daniel to one side. 'She's overshocked.'

'There was a lot of blood.'

'Well, there's bound to be if you cut yourself in the bath. The hot water makes the tiniest cut bleed like the devil.' He turned and looked at her, yawning and pale on the sofa, and said: 'The cut's nothing, but I think a night in hospital might be the thing, just to get her over this — shock.'

There was a dark blue light overhead and Connie, wearing a

41

white hospital nightgown, lay on her bed in the general ward. It was night, but women, some of them dressed, were wandering about or sitting on each other's beds talking quietly. Among their words were others and Connie heard a voice distinctly say, *'She's in the casual ward off Thrawl Street.'*

'Another voice said, *'You've got to stay the 48 hours. It's the law. She's gone to her sister.'*

'Which one?'

'You know. Across the river. They've been hop-picking.'

'Where's the money, then?'

'Drunk it, haven't they? She was drunk as a lord.'

'Here's tuppence, but not for rum. You look real poorly, Liz.'

A patient came up to Connie's bed and asked, 'What are you here for?'

'My kids were drowned when the pleasure steamer went down. I lost my old man.'

'You don't sound English.'

'I'm Swedish.'

'You're the worse for drink,' said another voice.

9

The next morning was dark and sodden. The windows and frosted-glass partition in the roof rattled with uneven bickering rain which, discovering the occasional hesitant slates, worried at them, nagged at them, until finally it dribbled between them. A patch in the corner of the ceiling started to darken and bulge.

They kept the hot white lights on and everybody, sick and well, turned a disturbing greenish colour. All around there was a powerful smell of wet rubber raincoats. Connie woke up feeling quite different. She felt all right. A young house doctor, his drenched hair sticking up in spikes, took her pulse and ordered commonplace drugs. She wanted to go. The depression was gone.

When Jane came to take her home at midday she was so full of energy, she said, 'Let's go and have a marvellous lunch. Let's go shopping. Let's walk across the heath.'

'Are you mad?' Jane's hand flew to her mouth. 'I mean, it's pouring with rain.'

'Oh, rain's lovely. It's soothing.'

Discomfited, Jane shifted from foot to foot. Then the old, how-to-handle-the-insane adage came to her rescue. Humour them.

'Well, all right. Let's.' Her enthusiasm seemed false even to someone accustomed to her noise.

Connie took Jane's arm affectionately. 'It's really nice of you to come and get me.'

'Well, I needed a day off.' Her voice was gruff.

'Is David O.K.?'

'Fine. My mother's there—will be there for some time. Much to Mark's dismay.'

'That cut was an exorcism. All the horrors leaked out of it.' She laughed.

43

Jane's expression was far from humourous. 'Well, don't rush things.' Mark had thrown another derangement into the ring—manic depression—and Jane felt he might have a point.

The summer leaves, swollen with rain, hung motionless like huge furry tongues. They made Jane feel quite disturbed and she was glad to get off the heath. They turned into the narrow streets leading to the top of Hampstead. Jane was talking about hi-fis and washing-up machines. She'd just got a deep freeze, and a washing-up machine was the new idol and new excuse for battle with Mark. 'Happened to call in at his bank on the way to get you and what do you think I find? There's two thousand quid in there. I'm not letting it rot while I spend half the day standing at the sink.'

Connie looked down. 'That's funny. The street's cobbled.'

'A lot are.' Jane eyed her suspiciously.

For a moment Connie felt badly shaken. Then she looked up—up into the grim sky—and said, 'Yes, a washing-up machine sounds a good thing but you still have to spend time loading it.' She took a noisy breath. 'Perhaps they should invent a machine for that.'

Obsessive, Jane decided.

The next street-corner was high up on a slope and there was a conspicuous shop, oddly shaped, painted black, that sold pottery. Connie could see a big floral jug in the window. Then it wasn't there. The shop wasn't there. It was night time. Nearby, men were singing drunkenly. She could hear a horse and cart coming along behind her. She screamed. 'There's a horse and cart behind me.'

Jane's voice cut in. 'Of course there's a horse and cart.'

Connie whirled round and the night time was gone. Coming up the splashy slope was a rag and bone man with his horse.

'I hope you've not come out too soon,' said Jane. 'You've gone a horrible colour.'

'It's probably the blood I lost. I'm all right.' She started talking quickly. 'We'll go to the new French place. We'll have lots of wine and garlic bread. I'd love onion soup, a steak—'

By the time she got to Heath Street her heart had stopped jumping and her colour was back. She walked effortlessly, enjoying the rain, and feeling good. People passing looked as though they thought her pretty, but she didn't feel quite as good as she had felt earlier. There was a shadow on her.

Connie and Jane sat on the sofa, and Daniel, undecided, paced between the arm chair and piano stool on the other side of the room. He passed two floor cushions, almost sat on the straight-backed chair in the corner but ended up for the third time at the drinks cabinet where he poured another large soothing whisky. Jane's hair was tied in a pony tail. Two racquets waited by the door. The bourgeois ordinariness of the room emphasised the barred windows, and Daniel, looking miserable, drew the curtains. It was a cold evening, the fire was on and Connie, watching the twinkling, twitching, flitting flames, said: 'I know it can't go on, Daniel. But don't you see, I say things I can't possibly have heard.'

'What do the voices sound like? Are they talking *to* you?' asked Jane.

Daniel left the room.

'No. They're just going on around me.' She spoke steadily. 'They sound normal until I realise what they're saying. No one I know speaks like that.'

'Is it like hearing them on a telephone?'

'More like a radio. They suddenly tune in, and then they're gone. Sometimes they're faint, but mostly they're just like you and me talking now. Do you know anything about possession, Jane?'

'I do,' said Daniel, back in the room. 'It doesn't exist.' He stared at Jane's thick white socks and went out again.

'That song I sang the night you came to dinner. How could I have known it?'

Jane, thinking back over that evening, said, 'Do you know Flower and Dean Street?'

Connie shook her head. She looked pale again.

'You said something about Flower and Dean Street. I remember the name.'

Connie, not aware she'd said anything, looked even paler.

'I've never heard of it,' said Jane.

They sat in silence.

'It was about the time of my birthday,' Connie said slowly. 'It all began then. It was something about that magician.'

'Oh, don't be ridiculous,' said Jane rudely. 'I admit he got

45

my watch strap being tight but — well, he also got lovers departing and approaching, didn't he?' She jigged her knees up and down. 'I suppose if you start tampering with all that magic stuff things could — get out of control, mixed up, all those vibrations flying about. Still I don't really believe it, any of it. You probably knew a Flower and Dean Street when you were a kid.'

'Probably,' Connie lied.

'It's a nice name.' She crossed to the bookcase, picked out the A-Z and turned to the index. 'It's here.' She crouched on the floor and her brown finger traced a squared map for some moments before she found it. 'It's a little street. It's in Whitechapel in the East End.'

'I've never been to the East End.'

'Perhaps when you were a kid . . .'

'Living in Brighton? Unlikely.'

Jane shivered. 'It seems extraordinary. It's probably a coincidence. Still . . .'

'Do you believe me, Jane?'

'I don't know.'

'Well, I know,' said Daniel, hurrying back to the whisky bottle. 'People say extraordinary things, do extraordinary things, clairvoyance, E.S.P., what you will. Yet when they're put to the test, the result is very ordinary. Nothing. It's not possible, so it doesn't exist.'

'Its not existing doesn't mean it isn't possible,' said Jane hotly. 'Fucking rationalist!' she said, as he went out.

'I'm going to find out what's happening to me and why,' said Connie bluntly.

'You'd better keep it from him. Balding, fat go-getter.'

They sat close together in Jivanjee Natraj's waiting room. It was very plush, and Jane whispered: 'The supernatural's on his side.' He appeared stealthily in the doorway, an exceptionally tall thin brown man, dressed in a well-cut grey suit. He bowed slightly but didn't speak, and Jane burst out laughing. Connie, giggly, embarrassed, followed him into his consulting room, where, still without speaking, he took her hands, covered the palms with blue marking-ink and pressed them flat on to some paper. He touched her shoulder lightly and she followed him

46

into a colourful cloakroom where he indicated a sink and she washed her hands. Back in his room he sat behind his enormous imitation Regency desk and pointed to a chair opposite. She sat down, which made her lower than him by about a foot. He put a pair of horn-rimmed spectacles on, and studied the imprints of her palms. 'Date of birth?' His voice, though soft, seemed to echo, and what he said stayed in the room.

She told him.

'You have an exceptionally good life with your husband. I see you are a good wife. Your life is tranquil, but you have an appetite for adventure.'

She looked surprised.

'In books.' He laughed. 'I see you like reading. The distinguished wife of a famous politician came to me yesterday. Like you, she is a good wife. Her eminent husband has many problems, but I am able to solve them. I help the Prime Minister of India. I help many people.' He pushed across a huge leather-bound book of press cuttings. 'Look. There is what the Prime Minister says about me. And here, the famous actor, celebrated all over the world — see what he says. I advise him on the roles he should accept.' He looked at the cutting hungrily. 'And here — see what they say about me in California.'

'Quite fantastic,' she said and snapped the book shut. 'Will I have any children?'

He laughed uproariously. 'You are participating in a trick, dear lady. You know you have four.' He looked back at the print. 'Your husband is very kind to you, most kind. He is well-suited to you.'

'Will I have any more children?'

Slightly uneasy, he looked out of the window. 'That is up to you, my dear lady. You have a decision to make soon. Please do not look so alarmed. It's about education. You have boy child, no?'

She nodded.

'You have your way about education, but you have to fight. Remember my advice and it will give you strength. You have a rosy future.' He smiled and his yellow teeth were stained and crooked. The smile gave his dignified face the crafty aspect of

47

a jackal. 'That will be seven pounds.'

She paid him and turned to go. His expression changed. He stared very hard and thoughtfully at her as she went to the door.

'What crap!' She imitated his voice. 'You have rosy future. You have boy child, no?' She laughed. 'What shall I do now?'

'Try another one.'

And they felt quite safe about trying another one.

10

Connie's bedroom was spacious and calm and reflected her serenity, her need for order. Daniel's personality didn't exist there at all. Rich blue curtains tumbled luxuriously on to the white wall-to-wall carpet. There was a full-length gilt-edged looking-glass. The lights were low except the one above the dressing table, where she sat, making up her face.

She mascaraed her lashes quickly, and then without thinking picked up an eyebrow pencil and emphasised her eyebrows. She unscrewed an unused rouge-pot and flooded her cheeks with colour. She painted her mouth. Dissatisfied, she searched for a darker lipstick. She picked up the pencil again and gave the eyebrows sensational arches. On impulse she enlarged her beauty spot. She packed her face with white powder, combed her hair so that it hung over one eye and gave Daniel the fright of his life. She seemed hardly aware of what she was doing.

'Cab, Connie.'

He managed not to say anything but silently repeated over and over the GP's number as though it was some mind-saving mantra. They walked to the gate, and he opened the door of the cab.

'Give my best to Jane.'

She got in and he shut the door. Loudly, she told the driver the name of a local cinema. Before they reached the corner she turned to wave, but Daniel had already disappeared.

As the cab turned left by the heath, she leaned forward and said, 'Take me instead to Flower and Dean Street, E.1.'

The cab throbbed at the corner of Fashion Street, while she walked up and down Flower and Dean Street. It was dark and cold and she had no feeling of recognition or anything else. Half the buildings had been pulled down. There was no one about. It was depressing.

49

She got back in the cab, and the driver said: 'Looking for anything special?'

'No.'

'It's all changed round here. All been torn down.'

'What was here before?'

'Houses.'

'Are any of the old parts still left?'

'I should think so. You ought to ask at the library.'

On Saturday evenings Connie and Daniel usually went to the home of Baxter, one of Daniel's colleagues on the council, and the routine was to have a drink and play mahjong. The following Saturday was Baxter's birthday and there were more people and more to drink. Daniel, his heart sinking, kept close to Connie; but she stayed sober, her make-up muted — she even seemed to enjoy herself. It gave him confidence to attend, as he'd hoped to, a meeting to try to pry the Lisson Grove derelict area out of the hands of the mad composition footballers.

At a quarter to twelve, Baxter came out with Connie to find her a taxi. He was older than Daniel, officious, hearty, with a loud voice and a clipped moustache.

'Dannyboy's a bit of a bounder with this Lisson Grove thing. He'll get his way. Wants half London torn down and his new hygienic — hey, cabbie!' He waved both arms.

'He likes getting things done,' she said loyally. 'Thanks for a lovely evening. Come to us next week.'

'Thanks, love, I will.'

The cab stopped, and he gave her address. He was just about to open the door when she said, '*Give us some money.*'

Taken aback, he fumbled in his pocket. 'Will a pound do?' Then he laughed. She was having a joke.

'*No, it will not do.*'

His smile died. If it was a joke, he didn't find it funny. 'Now come on, Connie —'

'*Come on, you bugger. Give us some more.*' She leaned sensually against the taxi and in the street light her face was coarse. '*Give us all you've got, big boy.*' She prodded him. '*All of it.*' She hiccoughed and giggled.

He pushed the pound into her hand, forced her into the cab, slammed the door and walked away fast.

Connie was preparing the Sunday lunch when the phone rang. Wiping her hands on her apron, she ran up to the hallway and answered it.

Baxter said, 'How are you?'

'How are you, Baxter? Isn't it a gorgeous day? It's spring again.'

'Terrific.'

'D'you want Daniel?'

'No. Is he there?'

'He's in the garden, pulling up the shrubs by the gate. People keep tripping up. I'll call him.'

'No. Look, Connie. I'm an old friend and I'm going to say something straight. Straight, anyway, is the only way to say it. Lay off the bottle. You can't take it.'

'But I hardly had anything.'

'I know. That's what's been worrying me until I remembered the ladies who carry gin in scent bottles. Lay off it, flower. It doesn't suit you. It isn't nice.' When she didn't answer, he said, 'D'you remember getting into the cab?'

'It's a bit hazy.'

'I bet it is. You were as tight as a tick.'

'Was I?' Her heart pounding, she sat on the stairs.

'You made me look a damn fool in front of the cabbie. You behaved just like a tart.'

Overcome, she put the phone down. David ran up with his bottle, then stopped and stared at her, worried.

'It's all right. It's all right,' she murmured. Then she grabbed him and held him to her, tightly.

11

Feeling rather silly, Jane and Connie sat in the kitchen of a small untidy house in the suburbs, while a little homely woman bustled about making tea.

'Is it a reading for both of you?'

'No. Only my friend,' said Jane. She dug Connie under the table and indicated her wedding-ring. Connie took it off.

'Well, I charge 15 shillings a reading—or should I say 75 pence as it is in the new money? Is that all right? I've had to put my prices up a bit, I'm afraid.'

'That's all right,' said Connie.

The woman beamed at her. 'Well, we'll get straight on, shall we? You don't look too well,' she said kindly. 'But I won't ask you any questions. Do you want your friend here, or would you prefer to be alone? She can sit in the living room. There's a good fire.'

'I'd rather she was here.'

The woman pulled up a chair and sat facing Connie, their knees almost touching, and instead of peering into the tea-leaves, as Connie had expected, she reached out, took Connie's hands in hers and then gently let them go. Her eyes were shut, as she settled back in her chair.

She shivered. 'Is it a cold day? I feel quite shivery suddenly. I expect you've come a long way.'

'Quite a long way,' Jane said brusquely.

'How did you get my name, dear? I only ask because I don't advertise, and I like to know how people come to me.' She spoke normally, but her eyes were still shut.

'From a girl who works with my friend—a teacher,' said Connie softly.

Jane looked at Connie as though to say, 'You're giving yourself away.'

'People come to me from all over. I don't see many people

any more as a rule, because I'm retired.' Connie, prepared for another failure, relaxed back in her chair. Then the woman said, 'But I thought I should see you. You probably wonder why I keep going on like this, but it's as though I want to get away from that shivery feeling. I think that's how you've been feeling lately. You keep doing things, going out, talking, you feel—oh, if I could only get back to the way it was before.'

'Yes.'

The woman's eyes were shut tight behind the thick pebble-glasses and she looked mottled, closed in like a tortoise.

'Are you afraid of gas lamps, dear? I know it sounds a silly question, but that's what I'm getting, so I have to ask you.'

'No.'

'Well, watch out for it, dear. I'm getting a lot of children here, oh, ever so many. Are they all yours? There's nine. No. You're too young. They don't have such big families as they used to. That's a funny thing to say, but I had to say it. Does it mean anything to you?'

'No.'

'There's a gentleman here, older than you. A father perhaps. Are you married? I have to ask. Otherwise what I say next is going to sound rather rude.'

Ignoring Jane's passionate signs she said, 'Yes, I am married', and she felt in her pocket for the ring.

'Well, I don't think I can really ask you anyway, because the question seems more for an older woman.'

'Please ask me.'

'Someone's asking how many half-pennies you got from the last bloke. It's funny, because half-pennies aren't used any more. It's funny as well because when I told you the price I said it in shillings, even though I've got so used to the new money I hardly ever make a mistake.' She spoke quickly, as though embarrassed. 'I feel you're running, but whether it's *from* someone or *to* them I can't see. You've not been well lately. It's not your body, more your—nerves. Have you been in hospital?'

Connie shook her head, forgetting completely the night she'd spent the month before.

'Have you got a dog? Well, I can see someone offering you one. You're not connected with the theatre, are you? I don't mean as an actress, more in the wardrobe department.'

'No.'

'I see a lot of costumes. Old-fashioned dresses and shawls and boots and bonnets. Perhaps you're going to get a job,' she said brightly. 'Do you wear gloves? No? I've got this older gentleman again. He's, oh — I get a feeling of irritation. If he gets a bit short with you, you mustn't mind. He's worried, but he doesn't know what to do. Is he a lot older than you?'

'Thirteen years.'

'Then he's not this gentleman I'm getting now, because this one's more your age. I see blackness all round this one. He comes out in the night. Does he work at night?'

'Her husband often goes out at night,' Jane cut in.

'I get a feeling of dissatisfaction. Is that your husband?'

'It might be.'

'Terrible dissatisfaction. Frustration. I think it's more this younger man. A job not finished. Does that mean anything to you?'

Connie shook her head.

'He doesn't wish you well, dear. I wish I could say he does.'

'Who is he?'

'He's too vague for me to see him. He's smart. Well turned out. He's a long way off.'

'Do I know him?'

'You have known him. Just once.'

The kitchen was suddenly very depressing. The woman stopped talking. Even Jane was still.

Then the woman said, making an effort to be cheerful, 'I get children going to school. I get only three. There should be four. One's not well and stays at home.'

'He's too young to go to school.'

'I think he should go to school. It would be better for him. Even a little nursery school.'

'Why?'

The woman seemed to hesitate, then she looked directly at Connie. 'When you're not too well, dear, it upsets him. I want to sing a song. Oh, it's ever such an old one.' She looked at her lap. 'It's even before my time.

> *'A smart and stylish girl you see,*
> *Belle of good society;*
> *Not too strict, but rather free*
> *Yet as right as right can be.*
> *Never forward, never bold*
> *Not too hot and not too cold.*
> *But the very thing I'm told*
> *That in your arms you'll like to hold.*
> *Ta-ra-ra-Boom-de-ay.'*

'My voice isn't very tuneful. You must excuse me. Does it mean anything to you?'

'No.'

'You haven't said anything about her future,' said Jane.

'Well, I can only see a little way ahead with anyone.' She looked at the window. 'Anyway, it looks as though it's brightened up a bit.'

They were both awake and staring into the dark.

'Connie,' he whispered.

'Yes. I can't sleep either.'

'I think we should go away, right away this summer. What about Spain? I could take my holiday earlier.'

'That would be lovely. But what about the summer-house for the back garden? You won't have the money for both.'

'I'll do that next year. Have you taken the pills the quack gave you?'

'Yes.'

'I'm sure you haven't. I wish you would. You're still depressed. They're supposed to be anti-depressants.'

'I'd like David to go to nursery school.'

'What?'

'I think he'd enjoy it.'

'Well—I—I'm not keen. No, Connie. We'll have to think about that.'

They lay silent again. She felt she was almost asleep at last when he suddenly turned and got on top of her and started kissing her, passionately. She didn't like it. The feeling got worse the more excited he got. She tried to sit up. She looked round her in the dark. She didn't know quite where she was.

The moment of alarm passed and she closed her eyes and relaxed. A different expression came into her face—lewd, cunning—and she murmured something sexually provocative, something a prostitute might say, something she couldn't have known. Daniel froze, then slapped her face hard.

Slowly he got off her and fumbled his way back to his place in the bed. They lay as before—separate, sleepless. Then she reached out and touched his hand and said, 'I'm sorry. I don't know what came over me. It felt different. I didn't know where I was.' She tried to laugh.

He didn't respond. She lay still, tears streaming down her face.

12

Six weeks after Connie cut her armpit, she had to go back to the doctor for a second tetanus injection and what he called a check-up. Daniel had been phoning him non-stop. Jane came with her.

The waiting room—it was also his drawing room—was lived-in and pleasant, with enormous sagging brown chairs like old dogs humped in front of the fire. There were only tattered magazines on knitting and housecraft, so Jane opened the bookcase.

'Do they go in for medical books! *The Aberrations of*—Can't pronounce it. Ah! This looks interesting. Crime. My God! The pictures. Ugh! "Her head had been nearly severed from her body, the womb and two thirds of the—"'

'Shut up!'

'"Had been pulled from her and left lying over her shoulder and—"'

'Will you shut up, you bitch!'

Jane looked up. 'Oh, I'm sorry. Christ! Is it upsetting you? I just thought—'

'I've got to get some new shoes.' Her voice was shrill. 'I want some red ones with—' Her foot tipped up. She stared at it.

Jane flopped on to a massive hairy chair, and its brown arms sank inwards and hugged her. She seemed quite unable not to read aloud. 'Lobe of her right ear missing? What could he have wanted that for? No one knew who he was, you know.'

'I don't want to hear, goddamn you, Jane!' Connie looked grey and drawn.

'He used to creep up behind them—Good God! They mention Flower and Dean Street.' Jane whipped over a page. 'Help! He did two in one night. Elizabeth Stride. Throat cut. No mutilation. Possibly because he'd been interrupted by a

57

hawker arriving with his horse and cart.' She leapt up, leaving the chair lopsided. 'Ah, here's an interesting one.'

'What does it say about that horse-and-cart one?'

'This girl's much more interesting. It took six hours in the mortuary to get her looking like a human—'

'Go back to the other one!' Connie's voice, low and desperate, was hardly recognisable.

Jane, resentful at being dragged away from an attractive victim, took a long time finding the page. 'Elizabeth Stride. Married in 1869 to a carpenter. Came from Sweden. In 1878, the pleasure steamer *Princess Alice* sank in the Thames and her husband and two of her nine children were drowned. She ended up in Flower and Dean Street, notorious for prostitutes, and was frequently arrested for being drunk. It doesn't say much.'

Connie murmured, 'Drowned . . . drowned.'

'Now with this other girl—'

'Go back to Elizabeth Stride. What about her death?'

'Just throat cut in Berners Street, 30th September, 1888. A hawker found her body at one a.m. . . . His horse shied with fright and probably disturbed the murderer who disappeared as if by some black magic before he could do anything worse. He had the desire, if that's the right word, to remove bits of the body. A labourer said he saw her with a man shortly before she died and the man said, "You'd say anything but your prayers". She was holding some grapes in her right hand and sweetmeats in the left.'

'A dissatisfied gentleman,' Connie said quietly.

'Where are you going? Hey, Connie.'

Connie was on the pavement by the time Jane caught up with her. 'What about your appointment? He needs, I mean wants, to see you. I'm sorry if I upset you. Heavens, you're a dreadful colour.' Connie seemed drained of blood—she could hardly walk. 'You are upset. I wouldn't have thought that would upset you.'

Connie insisted that Jane should go with her to Whitechapel; and Jane, although she said she thought it perverse, agreed. They took the 253 bus from Camden Town; it was a grey heavy afternoon and in that light Jane realised how Connie had changed. The laughter-lines at the corners of her eyes were wrinkles; her hair was lank; she no longer smelt of the summery perfume.

'God, you've lost weight,' said Jane.

Connie's face was washed out, the beauty spot glaring. She'd tried to go back to the clairvoyant in the suburbs, but when the woman knew who it was she said she'd definitely retired, most definitely. Connie had asked quickly, 'The man who didn't wish me well. Does he want to kill me?' And she had replied: 'I didn't get kill as much as steal.'

They trailed around the streets that had once been trailed around by the Ripper's victims, and Jane, who was carrying her long bag full of racquets, asked, 'Do you feel anything?'

Connie shook her head.

Jane stopped and took her arm. 'You've got to admit it's daft. We've done Flower and Dean Street twice, Berners Square three times.' She started giggling. 'I mean, if anyone knew what we'd been doing they'd lock us up.'

She laughed so much that Connie started too, and a man nearby stopped and stared at them.

'Perhaps he's the Ripper,' said Jane, and they doubled up, helpless with laughter.

13

The summer seemed full of heavy grey afternoons. One Sunday towards the end of July, Mark, Daniel and Connie sat by a tennis court watching Jane play. The club tournament — today the women's finals and Jane was winning. She was brown and lean, and she looked cooler than anyone around her, even the spectators. Connie watched Daniel watching her legs. It seemed to Connie that people had always noticed Jane's flat chest — *only* noticed her flat chest — but now suddenly it was her thighs. Her thighs were riveting. She put a hand on his arm, but he took no notice and went on watching Jane.

After the match silver cups were distributed, and everyone drank lemonade and escaped from the exhausting heat outside into the stuffy cool of the clubhouse. Kids whizzed round the long tables piled with sandwiches and lurid cakes. Jane pushed up to Daniel, showed him her cup and waited foolishly for his approval. Mark elbowed his way through the crowds towards her, said Congratulations and was ignored. He attempted to kiss her, but someone got in the way.

'It's got to go back to have my name engraved on it. I got the doubles as well.' She seemed weak with victory.

'It's a nice shape,' said Daniel. 'How does it feel to win?'

'Terrific,' and she hugged the cup.

As Connie was pouring lemonade for the children, she noticed Daniel in a corner, standing close to Jane, and it seemed to her that as they talked they were looking into each other's eyes.

The next morning, early, Jane came swinging up the path. Connie, wearing a bikini, was tidying the kitchen, and when she saw her, she bent down fast and hoped to creep to the stairs without being seen. She did not want to talk to Jane. It was another grey thick day and she was deeply depressed.

60

Too late. Jane's voice clattered into the kitchen. 'What are you doing?'

'Picking up something.'

'Can you have the kid tonight?'

They stood silently looking at each other. Without her racquet Jane looked vaguely unsatisfactory.

'Is Daniel in?'

Connie shook her head. Another silence.

'I just wondered if he could sort out a point of law for me. It's about HP,' she said breathlessly. 'I'm getting the washing-up machine on HP. It's the only way to get it. Mark makes Scrooge look like the Gulbenkian Foundation.' She started talking faster and louder. She hopped left-leg, right-leg, with an occasional yelp — she seemed much more her usual self.

'I'm going to track down that magician.'

'Oh no, Connie, don't! Don't be a fool. I mean, nothing's happened. I mean, the voices don't warn you of anything. Mark says it'll just wear off — vanish like poltergeists do. Anyway, I wouldn't go near a magician. There's a theory that the Ripper *was* a magician. He had to do five murders — the number 5 formed a pentagram — and then he'd be immune from discovery. He never was discovered . . . Mark and I are going through a real wobbler. We fought all night. At least I did. He won't. He locked himself in the kitchen. I've taken the key away. If he's not careful I'll take myself away. God, you're lucky you've never had anything awful in your life.'

'Will you help me find the magician?'

'No. I've got too much on my mind. I've got my own problems. Concentrate on what you've got going for you. I think Mark and I are — finished. I've got that feeling.'

Connie stared out thoughtfully at the grey day.

Connie went back to the nightclub. A fire door was open and the beam of afternoon light showed up the whirling dust and made the red plush chairs and little pink table-lights tawdry. The owner, tired and irritable, stood smoking a cigar and watching a chorus girls' audition. Connie, standing beside him, had finished her story and was waiting for a reply.

'Danchenko? Danchenko? He's not here.'

'Do you know where I can find him?'

'Why d'you want him? D'you want to book him?' He turned and looked at her.

'Yes. No.'

The man shrugged, and looked back at the girls. 'He's probably in New York.'

At the second theatrical agency a secretary said, 'He's not Hungarian. He comes from Tottenham. I can't give you his address, but he's appearing at the Spread Eagle in Barking.'

Seeing Connie's reaction, she added, 'It's his slack season.'

That evening Connie got the children to bed early and made chilled cucumber soup, cheese soufflé and a crisp salad. She put on her yellow backless dress and her new platform shoes and served dinner in their rarely used dining room. The sideboard was full of flowers from the garden. There were long candles in elegant holders and iced white wine.

As Daniel and Connie ate, they looked at each other from time to time but didn't once speak.

14

Connie was walking with David along a main road by the heath when a car slowed down beside them. She turned, and Daniel said, 'Get in.'

He drove to the nursery and they sat and watched as David knocked on the door and then turned and waved, smiling happily. They waved back.

'It can't go on,' he said.

She stared ahead.

'Bye, Mummy,' David called.

'It's not been right for weeks. We haven't made love, we haven't—'

'Well, you don't want to—'

'Nor do you. Not in your heart of hearts. We just avoid each other all the time—'

'You don't love me, Daniel.'

After a pause, he said, 'I do. Anyway, we've been together a long time.'

'What's that supposed to mean? I'm not tired of *you*.'

'Look, love.' He put his arm round her. 'I was put off the night you—well, you remember. I know I'll get over it. I'll certainly try. But you'll have to try. I think you should have analysis.'

'All right,' she sighed. 'All right. All right. Maybe I *am* nuts. I decided I must be the day we watched Jane play. I got terribly jealous. It was the way you were looking at her.'

'Oh, for heavensake, Jane!' He laughed.

'I got quite upset. I thought you were having an affair.'

He squeezed her to him. 'Well, let's you and me have a pact. You go to analysis and I won't look at Jane's thighs. O.K.?'

'Yes. I've never realised she had such lovely thighs.'

He stroked her hair, persuasively, and suddenly she grabbed his hand and kissed it.

'It's a lovely morning,' he said softly. 'You go and have a long walk on the heath. Enjoy it.'

Suddenly, marvellously happy, she walked across the heath in the sweet morning. The light was golden. A crocodile of school children moved noisily along a path to her left, a bumpy path that converged with hers by the lake. Today was the height of summer, with the heath over-ripe, full of scents and buzzings, the trees blowsy. Connie looked serene again. She moved at the same speed as the gnashing, swaying crocodile, its chattering so loud and shrill that it was impossible to distinguish anything, and they arrived at the lake together.

For a moment they muddled up. School children tried to pass Connie. She bumped into one, apologised and hurried to get ahead of them. Dazzled with sun, she stepped behind the old men with their fishing tackle and sandwiches, and the crocodile wound round, squeezed past the men and followed her. Among the shrill voices—were other shrill voices.

'Murder! Murder! He's done it again.'

Connie stopped.

'He's ripped her properly.'

The crocodile nudged up behind her. She ran, right to the top of the hill and over it, and flopped exhausted on to a bench. Below her, London was spread out misty and silent. She could see right across the river.

The crocodile came over the top of the hill and the children's voices rose up, again tinny and confused. Then she heard, *'Ripped out one kidney, whole. Ate it for his breakfast.'*

She jumped up and ran screaming down the hill.

The pub in Barking was brightly lit and had a very different atmosphere and clientele from the nightclub. Throughout the magician's act, the audience laughed uproarously. Instead of an MC an old woman, with a cracked voice, shuffled round touching objects.

'What am I touching?'

'A glass.'

'And now?'

'Another glass.'

'You can't fool Danchenko. And what am I holding now?'

'You are touching a bald head.'

The audience screamed with laughter.

'A glass.'

'What's in the glass?'

'Amber liquid. It won't be there long.'

'And now?'

'A looking-glass.'

'Wrong!' yelled the audience.

'Well, you know what I mean.' Caught off his guard, his accent was not the usual approximation to mid-European but a more familiar strain that came from no farther than Tottenham.

The old woman held her hand up as high as she could, but her bent body, stiff with rheumatism, deprived the action of drama, and the magician's response, sonorous, melo-dramatic—'Do not think you are touching nothing my friend. The air is not empty but full of vibrations'—made the audience roll about with laughter.

'She can't reach, Danchenko.'

'Want a bunk up, luv?'

The old woman lowered her arm and scuttled off into a corner. Danchenko, probably deciding that the supernatural stuff was getting nowhere with this audience, took off his blindfold and looked straight at Connie. 'He will not come like a thief in the night. And that means something to someone over there.' He circled a long finger and chose a woman at the back of the room. '*She* knows what it means.' And he added, addressing a fat woman by the bar, 'No lady. He's not under your bed.'

Wild laughter.

'Happy birthday to Alf behind the bar. 70 today.'

People cheered.

The magician looked at Connie. 'Now what have we here? The ideal couple? Ah, but only half of it tonight.'

'Her better half's gone off,' shouted a man nearby, and before the laughter entirely stopped, Danchenko said:

'And where's your heart this time, doomed lady? Not on your sleeve.'

'Go on. Make us laugh, Danchenko. Make us happy,' yelled the audience.

'Some people are too happy, my friends,' he said

65

maliciously, his eyes still on Connie. 'Some people are *too pure* of heart.' He accented the 'pure' and made it sound horrible. Then, rubbing his hands, he smiled round at the audience, and the smile, the most chilling thing so far, had quite the opposite effect to making them happy. The room was quiet as he took off his wizard's hat and gave it to the old woman. He leaned forward. 'Make sure you fill it up. Then Danchenko will show you a trick or two.'

As she took it round, Danchenko shouted abuse. 'Come on, you stingy swine. You miser. Your silver's in your other pocket. That's not enough, lady. I may be a magician but I can't live on air.'

The magician changed his clothes in the publican's cramped office on the first floor. A single naked light-bulb hanging from the middle of the ceiling showed up the peeling walls, the dust, the damp, the disorder. It seemed even to accentuate the smell — which was a mixture of stale beer, gin, fish and other less nice, less definable things. A cat had been sick on the soggy matting.

Connie, nervous but in control, knocked and went in without waiting for an answer. Danchenko, his thin body existing easily in the small space between a cluttered desk and a pile of beer crates, was taking off his make-up in front of a cracked mirror.

He twisted round, and they looked at each other, their eyes solemn in the gloomy room. Abruptly, he turned back to the mirror. He was not pleased to see her. His face changed with every layer he peeled off. He looked young, and then old and sinister, and then strangely naive. He stripped off the sides of his nose and wiped out his eyebrows; for a moment he looked like a professional tango-dancer from the 30s. Removing his wig, he revealed a head of black sleek hair, which he patted over with Brylcream.

'Why call me doomed?' she asked.

'I have nothing for you. The show's over.' The Hungarian accent was gone. He straightened up and seemed much taller than he did on the stage.

'Why doomed?' she asked angrily, and the desperation of the past months took away all fear.

'We are all doomed.'

'Why me?' she asked swiftly.

'Why me? Why me? Why not you?' he said in a sing-song voice. 'Why shouldn't anything happen to you? Why should you have everything?' He slithered out from between the desk and the crates and closed his black case.

'But I'm going to die.'

'Why shouldn't you die? People die violently everyday. Excuse me!' and carrying the case he slid past her and into the passage-way with all the ease and slipperiness of an eel.

She ran after him. From behind he looked young, sleek. 'It's my life!' she shouted.

He turned and said, scathingly, 'Why would *your* life belong to you?' He opened the exit door and turned left in the street.

Again she followed him. 'I'll run away. I'll hide. I'll stay in. I'll go abroad. I'll—'

He shook his head as he opened the door of the public bar. 'Whatever you do won't make any difference. It'll happen when you least expect it.'

He went in. The door swung shut.

Fleetingly, she saw him through the window leaning against the bar, a pint of beer in front of him. He looked malevolent.

15

It was a cold November night, and the station was ill-lit; but Daniel and Connie with Jane, Mark and several other friends were in high spirits and slightly drunk. They were waiting at the end of a short platform for the infrequent local train to take them back to London. The station was old-fashioned, neglected. A woman said to Mark, 'Some of these stations are early Victorian.'

'I love this line,' he replied mournfully. 'I hope they don't close it. They're always threatening to.'

'You've got that wrong,' said Jane. She hopped about and smiled at Connie. 'Soon be your birthday. Where shall we go? Soho?'

'It's what I've given the last two months of my life to do,' said Daniel. 'Tear down those old blocks. They're ugly. Of no historical value. Rip 'em up. Get rid of the squalor.'

'All at once?' asked Baxter.

'A clean cut of the knife . . .'

Connie shivered.

Jane hopped more energetically. 'Connie, I'm dying for a pee.'

'It's nice to see old Connie again,' said Baxter, thinking it was the last thing he wanted. She'd changed drastically. He'd decided it must be the booze. 'Where've you been hiding yourself?'

'Oh, I don't go out much. We don't entertain.' She looked cautiously at Daniel.

'You could hardly miss this evening,' he said. 'Daniel's victorious assault on big bogey itself.'

'Terrific darling!' Connie kissed him, but he didn't respond. He was looking at Jane.

'Come with me, Connie,' she said.

'The train's due in four minutes,' said Mark.

'Maybe it is, but you'll have a splashy patch on the platform.'

Connie moved close to Daniel, which put her under the light. Baxter decided her face was too pale. For an instant he thought of the terminal ward at the local hospital. He'd have to have a word with old Daniel about this.

Something made Connie look up, and she gasped.

'Why, it's a gas lamp,' said Baxter, pleased. 'You don't often see those.'

'Oh, these little stations often have them,' said Mark.

Connie moved out of the light, and her face, Baxter admitted with slight disappointment, was all right again.

'Isn't there a loo on the train?' asked the woman.

'No there is not,' snapped Jane. 'It's all that beer I've put back. I can't hold it. Come on,' and grabbing Connie she ran squealing to the waiting-room.

'Have one for me,' shouted Baxter.

It was locked up.

'Blast!' Jane scuttled to the ticket office. The collector was lolling by the entrance looking up the road.

'Where is it—the lav?'

'It's out of order. Best go to the pub, love.'

'Where? Where?'

'Just over there,' and he pointed up the street.

Jane and Connie started running.

'Can't hold it since I had the kid. A pint of bitter and I'm up all night.'

Making a strange growling noise, she dashed into the pub; and Connie was about to follow, when a group of people plunged out and sped towards the station. A train was approaching.

Connie waited on the corner, her black fur coat sleek around her and the light of the street lamp on her. She wasn't as beautiful as a year ago, but she was still appealing. The street—modern, suburban, with lighted shop-fronts further along—seemed deserted. She walked up and down, and then lounged on one leg and looked up idly at the sky.

Footsteps came up behind her. She froze. They were quite distinct on the stone-slab pavement. She began to walk fast in the direction she was facing, away from the station. The footsteps got faster. She started running. She could see a pub on the next corner. She could hear singing. Enormously relieved, she ran towards it. Though it was a cold night, a knot of people were standing outside drinking, and for some reason they stared at Connie. She looked at them. They didn't seem quite right. Their clothes were strange . . . She started running again, her hair falling forward over her eyes. She lost a shoe and looked down. The street was cobbled.

Gasping for breath, her chest aching, her legs numb, she stumbled on. She nearly fell. The footsteps, definite and slow, came right up behind her and stopped. In the distance, *'That in your arms you'd like to hold. Ta-ra-ra Boom-de-ay.'*

She turned, just slightly, and saw a shadow on the wall. She knew the shadow well. Then a man's voice — soft, educated — said, *'Now, my dear. You'd say anything but your prayers.'*

THE LOVE APPLE

1

Ken woke with the tight, fragile sensation of someone who is very ill, but he gradually realised that he only had a hangover.

The rain held the traffic noise down among the buildings and made sounds, streets away, seem clear. They collided in the soft cool room—retreating cars, loud splashing footsteps, clattering taxis. He couldn't move. The curtains, mauve and coarse, were filled with light.

Then he remembered the dog-food.

He twitched his toes wildly, whether to get relief from the menace of the dog food or to ease his hangover, he didn't know. His toes were the only part of him without pain, so the bored cat had to leap and strike.

'Bitch!' He flung his cigarette packet and missed.

He moved Christine's thigh off his stomach. Even in winter her skin was honey-coloured, her plentiful flesh firm.

He wiped a hand across his face and stood up, sickly.

His son Matthew greeted him with noise and demands. His dog had more sense.

Naked he rushed into the bathroom, locked the door and approached his hangover sternly. He took a short cold shower, a long cold drink, three aspirin. He did a swinging exercise and breathed deeply by an open window. For about two minutes he felt all right. Then he was obliged to lie down immediately—spread out, like a star fish.

His child banged on the door. 'Mummy wants bekfas.'

'Rubbish!' he murmured.

'Bekfas.'

'Matthew. Tell her to get her own.' His heart lurched up towards his throat again then turned right, as though to stabilize itself. He got up and spun into the kitchen. Coffee, strong and black, excited the alcohol, and nerves flashed and twitched.

He chose a pale blue shirt from the thirty hanging from the rail and a pink patterned tie. He brushed his hair, clipped his watch on and almost enviously watched Christine—she was sleeping again, serenely. Her body could deal with anything.

Christine's bath was running noisily and the smell of the bath salts filled the flat. The television was on, its sound turned down, and Mott the Hoople on the hi-fi thudded full-volume and could be heard three floors away. The phone was ringing—Christine, wearing a short transparent nightdress, was searching madly for a cigarette.

She had a lovely face that no amount of sleepless, wine-saturated nights seemed to ruin. Nights dried out by relentless smoking and drink left her bright-eyed, full of sturdy energy. They left Ken a ghastly green, unable to stand up or lie down, his body in bits and all of them painful. She, with the innocent cruelty of the strong, would say, 'Well, have another drink. What about some breakfast? You ought to eat something. Try a cold shower. A long walk.'

Her voice, with its careful vowels, was empty of personality, accent or flourish. It was quite deep and not unpleasant; but anything special about it had long ago been driven out by the elocution lessons of her youth. It was this voice that hinted at something she was only just beginning to discover—her lack of identity. As a remedy she'd tried painting, fashion design, writing plays. But she could never express herself or anything else.

Christine searched for cigarettes among the magazines and letters on Ken's side of the bed. She looked under his pillow, she prodded the bedclothes, she found them half-hidden by the sleeping cat. Matthew had answered the phone and was making delicate incomprehensible sounds, punctuated with uncooperative silences, much to the fury of the caller. Christine lit a cigarette, inhaled deeply, thankfully, padded back into the living-room and took the phone.

'Lilly! Lord! Fancy hearing from you! All this time! Very happy! Everything's marvellous. He's very happy. Just landed something really big. He'd got so much talent. Everyone says

74

so. Hang on. They're on.' She snatched off the hi-fi and turned up the telly for the ad break; she flopped back on to the low leather couch and Matthew threw himself on top of her. 'Got a bit of a hangover. What am I saying? A bit? It's frightful.'

The noise of the running water changed pitch. Then an ominous silence made her jump up.

'Hang on. Bath?'

When she came back the ads were over and she turned down the sound. She drank some black coffee and grabbed the phone.

'Yes, he's doing fantastically. What? Well, yes, we did have a bad patch, but that was ages ago, when I was expecting Matt. Fancy you hearing about that. He's fantastic. Very bright, like Ken. Everyone says so. He's got Ken's eyes. You know — hazel green, candid.' Her non-descript voice couldn't do justice to her enthusiasm. 'Come and see him. You must now you're back. I take Vit C and black coffee. No I never touch aspirin. Let's have a drink soon. Must go.'

She sat in the bath with Matthew, her long black hair hanging among the lemon bubbles, her big breasts floating on the water. She soaped Matthew's hair and drank some coffee. 'Head under, love.'

The phone rang. She heaved herself out and walked floppily into the living room.

'Pat! Hang on! Just get a fag. I'm feeling a bit shaky. Well, I should know better at my age. Broke all the rules, especially the golden one: I mixed them. Had two hours sleep. He's very happy. Just landed something incredible. I'd better not say yet. Hang on! They're on!' She reached over and turned up the adverts. 'Let's have lunch. Thursday's the only free day. Lovely. Bye.' She put the receiver down, and the phone rang again immediately.

'Jane! Fancy hearing from you. Everything's incredible. Ken has just got — what? I don't know much about them. I knew someone who sold refrigerators cheap but not deep-freezes. They fell off the back of a lorry. You know, wink wink! Ken's got — what? I didn't think you wore make-up. Well, there was a girl selling French products half-price but she seems to have gone off the scene. I'm very busy at the present because Ken's — O.K. Bye.' She smacked the receiver down hard. She'd got between the kitchen and living room and was almost in the bathroom when it rang again.

'Wendy! Fantastic! I thought you'd never come back. I don't go to the clubs any more. Ken doesn't dance. I'd rather not . . . I don't think he'd like it.' She leaned over and turned the schools programme down. 'I've only had one dress this autumn. Ken's had to have clothes. All the money's gone into the studio. I didn't have a coat till the second day it snowed. I don't seem to feel the cold. Yes, I did lose a bit of weight after Matthew but I've put it on again. Ken likes it. No. He never was one for the skinny birds.' She laughed. Her teeth were stained with nicotine. 'I must go. Matt's in the bath. He's only 19 months and he can talk. Isn't it incredible? Bye.'

Wearing a black silk bikini and a miniscule bra, she writhed on the green woolly floor. '29, 30, 31. Just a minute, Matt. Must get to 40, 33, 34.' She flopped, exhausted, and then stretched her legs straight into the air. Matthew was eating his cornflakes in front of the silent television. He croaked — the ads were on. She sat upright and got into a shaky lotus, sweat trickled, her heart raced. There seemed no earthly chance of her thighs ever lying flat against the floor. She pushed them disgustedly and stood up.

She was painting her toenails gold when it rang again.

'Liz, it was a marvellous evening. He's preoccupied at the moment. Lots of work, things happening. He's so clever . . . Yes, people are always telling me I should model. I haven't the time. Anyway, Ken wouldn't allow it. I wore a midnight-blue dress, boobs hanging out. No I wore it up. A great big old fashioned bun. People were knocked out. See you soon.'

She washed her face-pack off and quickly smeared on a gold glowing make-up. She curled her lashes and then got side-tracked by a faint line between her eyebrows. She massaged it, patted it; she didn't like it. Her mouth was wide, full and sensual. She painted it pink. Her eyes were large, beautifully shaped and soft. She surrounded them with silver eye liner and green and brown shadows and put a small red dot in the corner of each to bring out their colour. She talked gently, coaxingly to her son. 'Bye baby Bunting. Daddy's gone a hunting.'

She dressed him in his sheepskin coat, put him in his puschair and gave him an apple. She caught the dog and put him on a lead. She shook her only winter jacket, put it on and turned up the collar. She looked at herself quickly, unsatisfactorily, in the short mirror and they left the flat.

In the wet light the bright green carpet flowed through the rooms like a lush meadow. The cat pretended to graze but watched the corners with a wicked eye. The short mirror reflected the arctic bed, with all its rumpled, coiled sheets clean and sharp like a mountain range. It reflected Ken's long beaver-coat and one of his knee-length, hand-made, soft-leather boots, but could only catch half his rail of shirts. The mirror seemed starved. The rough mauve curtains flapped a little and the cat sat by the loud clock purring competitively. Everything was stylish, clean, admirable, but there was a solemn lonely air that wasn't allowed to exist when the rooms were occupied.

Then the phone started ringing.

2

'The media is the best way of reaching people.' It wasn't till half-way through the evening that Ken realised that Bunty was talking about television and not an opera.

Joel hurt his finger trying to crack nuts. In one hand he placed three Brazils and two cob nuts, but after several minutes of hard squeezing they stayed the same—firmly in their shells.

Bunty pushed over a saucer of peanuts. The enormous television was active in one corner, its sound turned down. Joel's face, a crafty oval in which everything sloped downwards, was unnaturally smooth. Ken suspected that he took hormones. He had long sensual lips. His currant eyes were too close to his nose and made him look dishonest. His hair was luxuriant black and styled to make up for the rest of him.

He flung two nuts into the air, caught them both and they disappeared into the podgy flesh of his right hand. He squeezed; his face became contorted; sweat covered his cheeks like dew. 'Goddam!' His manful act a failure, he reached for the nutcrackers and sat down.

'Television is where it's all happening. You can do so much. Also it's where the money is.' Her voice was innocent, light and full of laughter; it had nothing to do with the house, her husband or what she was saying. Despite her Grecian hairstyle and sophisticated clothes she was healthy and fresh and with her red cheeks she reminded him of a milkmaid in a child's picture-book.

Ken sat nonchalantly upright in an armchair facing the television. The way he lit his cigarette thrilled Bunty—all his movements precise and skilful. Ken was in command of himself and the situation. Joel was worried. He wasn't prepared for this intelligent, quick-thinking young man with a background. Dim, over-emotional types were what he liked.

Bunty nudged Joel and indicated the television. The ads were starting and he turned up the sound.

Ken leaned forward and watched intently. 'That's one of mine. The 95-second-cough-mixture is also mine but it comes on later.'

The ads over, Joel lowered the volume and wobbled silently across the room on his short legs. He drank a tumbler of orange crush and hit a nut spitefully with the end of a spoon. Then he started talking.

'It's like this, son. You work with me. I work with you.'

Ken moved a finger quickly, lightly, across his lips. It seemed to unsettle Bunty. She leaned forward, and for a moment it looked as though she was going to kiss him.

'The agency says you're a good guy. I like your cut-rate holidays. Bunty thinks you'd make anything appealing and she's got a good ear for a jingle. But you've a way to go yet. Your tune for breakfast cereals—too slow. You don't wake anyone up. I own three national food-packaging companies, a slice of two of the biggest recording companies, a string of hairdressing saloons—'

'Salons,' murmured Bunty.

'And a nursing agency.'

Ken caught sight of the emerald television grass and longed to escape—to be alone in a field, to smell real grass.

'You think, what the heck is a guy like Joel fooling around with nurses for. You say it's not a realistic idea: I gross over 100 percent.'

Ken lifted his eyebrows. He managed to satisfy even Joel without losing his dignity.

'What the hospitals pay in a week wouldn't cover a full treatment in my saloons. The girls get fed up and come to my agency. The hospitals are therefore understaffed. They've got to have nurses.' He spread his arms wide, leered and managed to look like the singing climax of a family musical. 'So where do they get them? I give their girls back for four times the original cost. The girls are happy. They also get tokens for a once-a-week hair-set-and-facial at any one of my saloons. This dog food is gonna be big, because everything I do is big.'

Ken looked at Joel's stomach bulging behind the pale green suit and tried not to laugh.

Joel swallowed another mouthful of orange crush. 'I know over here it's usual for the client to go to an agency and dump the whole project in their lap and let them get on with it. But I've got big by not being usual. Look at her!' He pinched Bunty's cheek. 'She could tell you a thing or two. She could tell you what she was before I found her and made her what she is now. Look at her. Isn't she beautiful?'

'Very,' murmured Ken.

Bunty's delight satisfied Joel and he padded back to his crush.

She turned to Ken, her expression quite different and said, 'I was a nurse in a geriatric ward.'

Ken smiled. He wondered whether it was there that she'd met her husband.

'I like to come in on the ground floor. Then when I see everything's Gung Ho I move on to something else. Now, what have you got up your sleeve for our lucky doggie *amigos*?'

'One or two things. I'm against a vocal.'

Joel nodded, his currant eyes full of sly assessments.

'Quick, they're on.' Bunty stood by the television in all her full-blown shapeliness.

'Put your ideas on tape and bring them straight up.'

'I think the agency would feel a bit left out.'

'Let them feel left out. He who calls the piper. You'll get percentage of the brand image—'

'Repeat money?'

'The usual percentage. Contract negotiable after nine months. It'll take six to get it going. After two years, if it goes, a new ad. Plus'—he lifted a cautionary hand—'a percentage of the foreign market.'

'What length?'

'75 second. I aim to push it. Maximum exposure. A hundred-piece orchestra, a set of African bongowallas—whatever you want for your jingle you'll have it. I'm not mean. You stick with me, Kenneth, and I'll get you to Venice. Stick with me and you'll get the Golden Lion.'

He celebrated Ken's perfunctory nod with a further glass of crush.

Bunty poured Ken another Scotch and looked with yearning at the silent horror movie. Joel, his long flat feet splayed at a sensational angle, shuffled business papers on top of the grand piano. He held up a blue flimsy sheet covered with figures. Ken wondered what his legs were stuffed with.

'There's lots of dog-foods. Ours has to be different.'

'Where'd you go to school, son?' Joel's voice was sharp.

Ken named a well-known public school. It was lost on Joel. 'After that?'

'Oxford.'

'What degree did you get?' All his questions quick as gunfire.

'A second.'

'What in?'

'History.'

'You wrote the music for a revue?'

'No, I wrote an opera. It was performed at Glyndebourne and—'

'Only child?'

'It was based on Kafka's *The Castle*.' He lit a cigarette. Through the smoke, his eyes were hard. 'I am an only child, yes.'

'Married?'

'Yes.'

'How many times?'

A slight hesitation. 'Three.'

'Think this one'll stick?'

'I mean it to.'

'What went wrong with the others?'

'I walked out.'

'Bored?'

'I felt like it. That's why.' He was furious.

'Joel! Look at his eyes. Aren't they something?'

A laugh escaped from Joel and didn't get far. 'You should have been in movies.'

Ken managed to smile. Actors bored him to death, but he didn't feel it appropriate to say so.

'Any kids?'

'I've got—'

'D'you play around or stick with the wife?' He looked at Bunty.

'I write background music reasonably well. You know that.

My private life is my own.'

Joel stroked Bunty's ringlets. 'You're beautiful.'

She flushed and didn't deny it.

Joel bent lower and his face bulged—it frightened Ken. Bunty was used to it.

Joel was swollen with crush and looked about to burst, but he still managed to swill down another half-tumbler. 'Have another, boy', he said, and waddled over with the scotch.

'No thanks.'

'Come on, come on.'

'No really.'

The bottle still pushed towards him and he put a hand over his glass, quickly. 'I don't want one!' All his consonants snapping.

Defeated, Joel stood the bottle on the piano. 'Not a big drinker?'

'Now and then.'

'The agency said you're 32.'

'They don't usually lie.'

'You play a close hand, son.'

'Look at that muck you drink! Sugary muck! There's no oranges in it, that you can be sure,' said Bunty.

'Where do you come from?' Ken asked her.

'I was brought up in the country. Somerset.' Her voice soothed his hangover. She was fresh, clean, full of delight. He'd rarely seen delight, except in children.

'It's slimming, honey.' Joel's eyes grew round, looked hurt.

'Slimming! It's all white sugar, saccharine and flavouring. It'll kill him one day.'

Ken smiled at her, his first real smile.

'Now let's get on with the graft,' said Joel. 'Name, image, presentation, price.'

'Isn't that the copy-writer's problem?'

'Poop!'

'Good name,' said Bunty. 'That's about what it'll be too.'

'Rover. I'm in favour of Rover.'

Bunty and Ken looked at him. Their mouths didn't quite hang open.

'Well, come on. I throw it at you. Throw something back. How about Rover, son?'

'How about Munch?'

'Or Crunch?' said Bunty.

'Brunch!' Joel's little eyes shone. Steam rose from his amphibious body. 'Brunch it is.'

'That's a good one, Bunty,' and Ken winked at her.

'Dangerous,' she murmured and then said loudly: 'Not everyone has telly. I mean some ignorant human being might just miss your 75-second ad and eat it himself.'

'There'll be a dog on the tin, presumably,' said Ken. 'Why not call it "Doggy Brunch", just to make sure there's no confusion?'

'Mongrel or pedigree?' asked Joel.

'Pedigree on the expensive version, mongrel on the cheap. Market two brands,' said Ken.

'We're getting there.'

'Champ!' said Bunty, softly. 'I like an evocative name.'

'Give a dog a challenge,' said Ken. 'Not the usual wet slop. Real bones and gristle. Do it in grades. Get them to grade the congealed rats or whatever they use.'

'I like it,' breathed Joel.

'Champ. Only if your dog's really a dog! Gives a dog staying power.' Bunty looked at Ken. 'Champ for the dog who knows his business.'

'What about Tramp?' asked Joel, his voice icy.

'Come on. You can't have that in dog-food,' said Ken.

'Or Lash,' said Joel.

Bunty did not look pleased. Ken thought Joel must be touching on some unsavoury conjugal twist.

'What's your wife like, Kenneth?' asked Joel. 'I bet she's beautiful and petite.'

'What about Potent?' murmured Bunty. 'For the dog who can't make it.'

Joel made a nasty growling noise and it looked as though he'd hit her.

'Snap!' said Ken quickly. 'Call it Snap! What d'you think, Joel?'

'I like Brunch. It's wholesome.'

'Gay dog,' said Bunty, giggling.

'Is your dog big enough for Snap?' said Ken, suddenly fed up. 'Is your dog dog enough for Snap? Fill it with bones and dead cats. In a flap get Snap. Gives a dog balls. No crap with Snap. Market several brands. Crapping Snap, Lullaby Snap, Action Snap. You can subtitle that one "Charver". Is your dog aroused? Does your dog get it?'

Bunty gazed at him, her mouth open.

Joel, uncertain how to take this, murmured, 'Quick bite.'

'You could have a slimming one,' said Ken, thinking he'd please him.

'I still like—'

'Snap with the built-in laxative. Snap makes them crap. Or alternatively, No crap get Snap. Snap cures clap.'

Uncontrollably silly, he stood up. 'That's it. Snap cures clap: 20p. Charver for the dog who likes oats: 35p.' He went to the front door, which had enough stained-glass for a small church.

'The street will be littered with canine sex maniacs,' said Joel miserably. 'It's bad enough with the crap.' He followed Ken, his hands flapping, 'Stay. Stay.'

'No.'

'But it's only nine.'

Ken opened the door.

'Once I've done the ground work, you're on your own,' Joel threatened.

Ken hurried down the steps. 'Just this one then I'll stop,' he said to himself. He jumped into his car and drove away fast, without looking back.

Snap cures clap. He couldn't get it out of his mind.

3

Meanwhile Christine, wearing a sensational make-up and long black evening gown, sat on the bumptious black couch watching the silent television. Beside her a bottle of cheap wine, almost empty, and a saucer overflowing with cigarette ends. She removed her gold choker — it was too tight — and looked again at the clock. Her full mouth was hard and determined.

Matthew hurtled, out of control, after the fleeing cat. The phone rang. Christine sighed enormously and her flesh quivered. She picked up the receiver and nonchalantly said, 'Yes? — Wendy! — Oh!' Her voice dropped and died. Disappointment forced her to drink straight from the bottle as she sat, silent, morose, not listening, the phone pressed against her ear. 'Do you have the right time?' she asked suddenly. 'No. It's just that he's seeing some business people — really important — and I thought he'd ring or something. I thought he'd book a table somewhere to celebrate. I suppose now we'll have to go for a late supper. Just a minute.' She grappled with the phone and the bottle and managed to turn up the ads without leaving the couch. 'No nothing wrong. Bye.'

She watched the crisps ad, the 20-second-soup, the de-luxe-aspirin.

'Be quiet Matt. It's one of Daddy's.'

The phone cut into the sexy cigar 75 seconds and she snatched up the receiver.

'Yes?' She wasn't quite as nonchalant. 'Jane! You are a funny lady. I don't see you or hear from you for months and then you ring twice in one day. Just seen two of Ken's. Hold on!'

She put the receiver on the couch and Jane carried on talking. She went into the kitchen, poured a glass of water and went back to the phone. She listened to Jane and looked at her gold nails. Eventually, 'I haven't seen the refrigerator man,

85

Jane, not for ages, not since I got mine. I'll try and find his number for you,' she said tolerantly. It would take more than Jane to inflame her nerves.

Christine ate a family-size can of soup that Ken had put to music, but not quite the way they did on the ad. She ate savagely from the saucepan, wiping it dry with huge crusts of forbidden bread.

Eleven o'clock, and it seemed obvious to her that, as he hadn't invited her to meet the dog-food people and celebrate, he'd bring them back for a drink. It would be too humiliating to be found dressed up, waiting to go out. She saw Matthew's bar of milk chocolate on the high shelf and, in spite of 'best intentions' and 'think slim,' ate one square. It comforted her. She allowed herself two more and then left the self-abusing haven of the kitchen and changed into a white lace nightdress. She let her hair down, took off her pearl chandelier ear-rings and tried to look relaxed. 11.25. She finished the chocolate bar and phoned Ken's assistant.

Frances was a polite intelligent girl of 27 who lived alone and liked cats. She was rather plain, wore no make-up, had taken a first in English at Cambridge and didn't seem part of the ad world at all. Ken liked her because she was clear-thinking and bright. Christine liked her because she was no competition.

Christine apologised for waking her and asked where Ken was. Frances didn't know. Her voice was calm and classless.

Christine looked at her nails and saw that the gold was chipping. Her legs, she realised morbidly, were filling up again with small hairs. 11.30. She was full of imperfections.

'I don't think he's crashed the car,' said Frances, quite humorously. 'However drunk he is, he always sobers up when he's put in front of the wheel.'

'Well, I'd have liked at least the chance of getting drunk with him.'

'Do something till he gets in. Can't you read?'

Frances realised with horror that in Christine's case the more literal meaning might well apply. 'Or look at magazines,' she added quickly.

'He always gives me books but I start them and don't seem to finish them. He gave me *Portrait of an Artist* by James Joyce but I can't really get into it. I don't understand it. What's it really about?'

'It's about how an artist has to escape his own history and culture in order to achieve the state of exile which is the fundamental condition of art itself.'

'Oh, you are clever Frances. I must go. I must do my nails before he gets in.'

She stood naked in front of the dead television set and massaged her body with a warm perfumed oil. It seemed to soothe her. She did fifty floor exercises — ten more than usual to punish the white bread and chocolate. She put on some gold Hollywood-style pyjamas, bright and stiff as tin foil, and climbed on to her scarlet platform-shoes that looked not unlike two skyscrapers in a sunset. She'd just decided to step down again, take off the tin foil and wear nothing except a black leather choker, when keys shook outside and he came in.

He was sober. Looking at him made her forget all the uneasiness of the evening. She wanted to touch him. She was dying to touch him.

He flung himself on to the steel-framed black-leather chair and stretched his legs. Was he in a bad mood or a good mood? She hovered by the television set and might as well have been dressed in a hospital operating-gown for all the notice he took of her.

'Where's the dog?' he asked.

'In our room, asleep.'

'Has he been out?'

'I took him at 6.30. How did it go?'

He shrugged.

'You haven't got it?' Her voice trembled.

'Yes, I've got it. I'm just tired. What have you been doing?'

'I read *Portrait of an Artist*. I like the way it deals with art and exile.'

He laughed. 'Don't you mean it's really a form of religious epiphany?'

She wobbled uneasily on her skyscrapers and looked at the floor, her face burning, eyes sullen, like a schoolgirl who has been caught cheating. She bit her nails and the new scarlet lacquer shivered and cracked.

87

'Who's been educating you?'

'Only you.' She added timidly, 'It seemed very vivid about being a boy and growing up in Dublin.'

He smiled suddenly and held out his hand. She rushed across and took it, took him, held him. She was where she wanted to be and he, as on the floor he rolled with her, thought that some real composing would be the only salve for his dejection but he was too tired.

4

His mother lived in a thirty-roomed house at the top of Highgate, with one servant, a gardener and a dwindling collection of Picassos. She was bent over, her nose almost brushing the carpet, with the weight of a hundred imaginary ailments. Her only actual one—lunacy—she didn't pay attention to at all. She entertained important people, hid money in flower pots and was reputed to give guests dog biscuits for tea. Ken's gentle father had been dead three years. She'd killed him. She'd used several methods—none of them illegal.

'How's the synthetic jungle?' Her voice was like gravel. She tried to kiss him but he'd learned to avoid that long ago. 'We had an interesting evening. A gallery-owner from New York talked about Ernst. You'd have enjoyed it. The Rothschilds were here. You should have brought, what's her name, your assistant, Frances.'

He by-passed the tea table with its Georgian tea service and unique sugar bowl. A few cafeteria custard tarts were arranged in a silver dish and looked as though they should be taken out of the sun before they became actually dangerous. There was a pink-and-brown jam roll—he'd seen it before. He almost admired the way she got away with it.

He phoned Christine. The number was engaged.

'I'm off to Buck House Friday,' his mother said. 'I don't know what to wear.'

As she always wore the same clothes, a long black brocade dress slit to the thigh, the slit possibly not intentional, laddered black stockings reaching just above her knees and a rancid yellow fur like a dead tom cat, he didn't give the matter any thought. He tried Christine again.

'Perhaps I should get Hardy to do me something. Or I could wear the grey silk.'

'Don't,' he advised. 'And please don't wear that black brocade. It looks like two curtains sewn together—badly.'

She looked up at him, her black eyes burning with what he always took to be madness. She laughed suddenly, showing teeth no dentist could cure.

'What are you doing?'

'I'm writing the background music for an all-purpose, ninety-percent-gristle dog-food.'

'Give me a cigarette.'

He snapped his lighter under her nose and snapped back into position, out of her reach.

'Laura's back from L.A. She's finished the film. She looks glorious. She'd like to see you.'

He went back to the phone and dialled Christine. Her voice was breathless and he thought she must be in the middle of her pelvis control swing. 'Shall we go to the White Tower and celebrate?' she said immediately.

'I can't tonight. I'm going out.'

'Where?' she asked desperately, and then corrected herself and in a softer tone added, 'Where to?'

He sighed. 'I'm taking the dog-food pair to dinner.'

'But you went to dinner with them last night.'

'No,' he said curtly and looked at his watch. Because her phone had been engaged he'd overstayed the visiting time. 'I've got to go. I'll see you.'

'But you didn't come in till twelve. What d'you mean, no dinner? Are they on a fast?'

'I left before dinner, Christine.' Pause. 'I just walked about. I needed to think about it.' Hurt, shocked intake of breath.

Behind him his mother chuckled, a rich jolly sound. Not all her humour was in a minor key. He'd forgotten to keep her in sight and turned quickly. She was rubbing her butcher's arms.

'I can't get out of it, Christine. And I'll have to take them to a little place afterwards. So I may be late.'

She didn't reply and he sighed again. He was embarrassed by Christine—by her stupidity, the way she walked—and he hated himself for being so. Her expansive flesh did not make up for her narrow mind.

His mother swooped—powerful, dangerous. He thought she was going to grab the phone, so he jumped back; but she was only reaching for a cake.

'I wish you wouldn't conduct your domestic squabbles with that woman in my house.' She used that imperious dinner-table voice which made even the most socially-assured tremble. He stared back, pink with fury.

'Why do you have to go on somewhere?' Christine asked.

'Because dinner will be short.' He tried to speak gently. 'They're both on diets, strict diets.' He looked at his watch. He was out of the safe period and well into danger time. 'I saw Jane, the gym mistress, in the street this morning, and she told me about a magician at one of the West End clubs. She said he's rather spooky. He sounds all right. The dog-food pair look as though they like entertainment.'

As he hadn't invited her, she supposed correctly that he didn't want her, but she couldn't stop herself saying, almost childishly, 'Shall I come?'

'Oh love.' He sighed noisily. 'It's business.'

And so began the era of, 'It's business.'

'See you next week, mother.'

'Doctor Williams just came by. He brought a specialist to look at my kidneys. My gall bladder's causing the trouble. It's playing havoc with my whole body. I told him so.'

'I'll go now, Mother. Then you can straighten up.' He'd never believed in the boomerang.

5

He sat between Bunty and Joel and looked absently at the lively breasts and tired eyes of the show girls. Bunty was wearing a black lace gown and her smile was saucy. He loved her bright cheeks, and the way they dimpled. She smelt, but not of perfume. It was a private smell, reminding him of fresh-cut grass and country mornings.

'And how's Clap curing Snap?' she asked. 'Joel likes you. Yes, he does,' she protested, as though he'd denied it. He hadn't. He was used to people liking him.

The MC came on and Joel relaxed in the quilted chair, his stomach swelling freely like a balloon.

'Hate dogs. Hate them!' he said to Ken. 'Can't stand their doggy breath. I'm going to invent a gun to put them down anywhere, anytime. It'll be shaped like a pointer's head and it barks as it fires.' His powder and rouge stood out in the pulsing light. He was wearing more make-up than his wife, Ken realised. 'Detestable, fawning creatures. Read about a guy giving his dog the kiss of life. Can you imagine? Mouth to mouth with a dog.'

'I like dogs,' said Ken. 'But I don't think I'd go quite as far as that.'

'Where's your wife?' asked Joel.

'She's busy.'

'Joel says you've got a positive chin. You'll go a long way. He likes that.'

'And now for your exclusive entertainment we have the proud pleasure to present the greatest magician in the world — Danchenko.'

Ken recrossed his legs. His hair was standing up, boyishly.

'Snap will put you on the map,' Joel told him.

Doves flew about and chiffon scarves multiplied in a boring way. Ken thought guiltily of Christine. He'd love to show her off if only she'd shut up.

Joel watched the magician. 'You could learn something from his eye make-up,' he told Bunty.

'So could you, darling,' she replied.

The three-ball juggling act reminded Ken of a pawnbroker and he shivered a little, for in spite of his bank balance — his mother's bank balance — the fear of being broke was always lurking at the back of every triumph. 'Has the agency agreed the contract?' he asked Joel.

'Sure,' said Joel, and looking at the magician, 'I wonder how he keeps so slim. It's almost magical.'

'Why don't you hire him for your calorie-free cornflakes?' said Bunty.

Joel's braying laughter surprised the silent, concentrating audience, and people looked round at him, rudely.

Roll of drums. 'And now Danchenko will identify any object you choose.'

The MC stretched up and was about to blindfold him with the first of three thick scarves, when the magician turned sharply, his eyes glittering, in the direction of Joel's table. Had the American's inappropriate laughter offended him? The audience stared. Joel, thinking his business acumen was about to be publicly recognised, waved a cheery hand.

Then the magician saw Ken.

For a moment he seemed to stagger on his tall box, his black clothes flapping piteously. 'O.K. Dan?' the MC was heard to murmur. The magician still stared, his face pale. Then he looked as though he wanted to run away.

An impromptu roll of drums seemed to pull him together. A man at the next table leaned towards Ken. 'Are you the law or something?'

'No, this boy's doing our new dog-food jingle and the magician's giving us a build up,' said Joel. 'He'll start barking next.'

Bunty was amused and her laugh tinkled like bells.

Ken leaned towards her. 'I like the way you laugh.'

'It's called Snap,' said Joel loudly.

'Not once, not twice, but three times for Danchenko!' The magician was blindfolded. His long clothes quivered as though his legs were shaking.

The MC swished one way, then another, through the tables.

He picked up a glass. 'What have I here, Danchenko?'

'A glass.'

'And now?'

'Another glass.' His voice was unsteady.

The MC moved towards Ken's table and the magician raised a hand as though to guard his face. The MC picked up a lump of ice. 'And now?'

'You are touching a bald head.'

'No!' shouted the audience.

'It was bald once,' replied the magician.

Slow hand-clap. The MC dropped the ice in the bucket and took the evening bag Bunty held out.

'A soft suede bag with a jewelled clasp.'

'Right' Joel shouted. 'Isn't he terrific? Isn't that marvellous?' and he clapped loudly.

'Ken, give him something of yours—quick!' said Bunty.

He shook his key ring at the MC.

'You've got access to a lot of places,' said Bunty. 'They can't all be to your front door.'

'Studio, my car—'

The MC took the keys and held them high. The magician tried to speak. Then there was silence.

'He doesn't know,' said Joel. 'I'll give you a clue. What d'you get at twenty-one?'

Laughter.

'Blades,' said the magician, his voice resigned.

'Wrong!' shouted the audience.

'No, he's right,' said Ken softly. 'My silver pen-knife's on there.'

'They're of different sizes. One's curved, another's long and pointed.'

The magician carried on, each word resigned, without question. 'Then there's the one that gives joy. It cuts deep to release the spirit. Next.'

The MC gave the keys back and moved to the next able. 'What am I holding?'

'A glass.'

An embarrassed silence. He was holding a napkin.

The magician wrenched off the scarves and looked straight at Ken. 'I can't—I can't go on. I'm sorry.'

94

He got off the box as the MC rushed on to the stage and they almost collided. 'I regret deeply that the great master is a little unwell. He will do a small performance of juggling.' The MC gave him the hoops.

'I'm sorry about this,' Ken told Joel. 'He was supposed to be good.'

'Joel was only a stage in my life,' Bunty said in his ear. Ken decided she'd got her tenses muddled up.

Hoops spun in the air for some time. Then one dropped with a spiteful clatter and rolled off into the audience.

'I love it when it goes wrong,' said Joel, laughing loudly. 'It's much more fun.'

Ken got up. 'Come on. This is too awful. Let's get a drink somewhere.' His long legs moved swiftly and Joel had to wobble fast to keep up with him.

'First time he's been like this,' said a man by the exit.

He woke up suddenly in the grey dawn. Like love affairs, his hangovers were never familiar. His heart throbbed. Everything felt sickly and shaking, and behind this horror was something else. The noise outside seemed louder than it should—heavy wooden wheels and horses' hooves and shouting. He opened his eyes. He had no idea where he was. He couldn't remember anything, he couldn't anticipate anything. There was one thought in his mind—he must get out of London.

He felt dull, strangely satiated and disgusted. And he felt frightened.

Then on his arm he saw something—it was on his chest as well—a dark awful stain. He sat up and started rubbing it violently, but when he took his hand away it was still there. 'I'm covered in it, for Godsake. It's all over me.' His head was so full of horror he shut his eyes and covered his ears. Then he heard a voice.

'You're still drunk.'

'It's all over me.'

'What?'

'I'm covered in blood.'

'Where?' Christine jolted up. Eyes closed, he was rubbing his arm again.

Christine's voice. 'That's not blood. It's the way the light

95

falls.'

He opened his eyes and saw dark shadows from the mauve curtains falling across his body.

'You're still drunk, Ken.'

'Was I very pissed?'

'Can't you remember? No. I suppose you can't.'

He could hear Joel say, 'Snap will put you on the map.'

He sat on the low leather couch drinking heart-whizzing black coffee. Everything was low in the living-room and he said, 'Can't we have some normal-sized furniture?'

'Can't we have some money to get it? You said you liked this.'

Her eye make-up was smudged and she looked like a Panda. She was smoking already and in a horrible mood.

'You look vile,' she told him.

He picked at his jacket, nervously, and tried to remember which was the aspirin with the irreversible side-effects. He'd already had four, but pain was still gnawing in his head. His stomach, a poisonous swill, would accept no more coffee.

'You're very quiet about last night,' she said.

'The act was a mess.'

'Well, I'd hardly know, darling, as I wasn't allowed to meet them.'

'For Godsake, I didn't want to have to sit through that rubbish.'

'You make them sound so attractive.'

'You wouldn't have enjoyed it. It's business.'

'What are you doing today?'

He had to go away, and he almost said, 'I must get out of London.' Then he remembered his studio.

'Is the dog-food woman beautiful?'

'No. She is not beautiful. Is there a riding-school near here?'

'No.'

'I'm sure I heard horses this morning.'

'Oh, do shut up.'

'I did. I remember smelling horse crap.'

He could also still smell blood, very slightly.

6

With the first cheque he bought a white Porsche and he and
the dog purred round London. The jingle was everywhere—
even his child was singing it. Christine phoned the studio
non-stop. 'It came on twice before seven and in each break
during the film.' His whole world shook to the tune of Snap.

One afternoon, he stood with Christine and Frances in
Kensington High Street. They'd just had lunch and he was
lighting their cigarettes. Suddenly a crowd rushed towards
him, shouting, arms waving. He stared, appalled, and then
turned and ran.

He ran for almost a mile in and out of the small streets, and
when finally he stopped, ill with exhaustion, in a doorway, he
had no idea why he'd done it. He was still frightened.

Christine and Frances looked at each other, baffled.

The shouting crowd caught the escaping bus, forced it to
stop and got on.

The studio was a converted greengrocers in North London,
and attached to it was a beautiful Victorian conservatory,
which Ken used to store equipment. He repainted the studio
silver and put gold stars on the ceiling. Pictures of Christine
stayed, but photos of pop groups were out. He inspected the
new 3,000-pound machine which could create any sound, or
combination of sounds, imaginable. He pressed keys and
buttons for almost an hour.

'Make a cow mooing,' said Gordon, his second assistant.
'Can it do the squelch of an unblocked sink?'

'Can it do the sound of success?' Joel was suddenly in the
studio. He looked at the flickering, many-eyed enigma and
said, 'It's got to pay its way, same as everything else on my
payroll.'

'It'll save time,' said Ken. 'It's the best on the market.'

'Slimming Snap's hitting it right. A lot of it's the long thin tin.' Joel's face swelled, eyes popped. He was becoming enthusiastic and as he had a talent for making most energetic states malevolent, Ken dreaded his enthusiasm. 'I want to bring up the proteins.'

'Careful of your Trade Descriptions Act,' said Ken.

'I want you to put in a bar or two of protein music.'

'What do proteins sound like?'

'I don't know. Healthy, bouncy, light. It's up to you, boys. You're the artists.'

Ken left Gordon in charge of the latest cough-mixture-40-seconds, got into his Porsche and sped towards the motorway.

He felt empty, yet full of desire. He supposed that that was what success was. He didn't know what he wanted. He thought he wanted Christine's big breasts, her strength, and rushed home.

'I'm sorry.'

Her excitement shut out his soft confession. She bit his ear, gripped his back with her thighs. Her teeth pricked up and down his neck. Her skin was hot.

'I'm sorry. I can't.' He drew away from her and supported himself on his arms. She waited, eyes shut, for him to begin.

She waited and everything subsided enough for her to open her eyes. He was looking at the window, and what was more surprising, he was obviously not aroused.

'Have you . . . already?' She was still breathless.

He shook his head, climbed away from her and lay on his side. Christine had too much sense to pursue him, and she waited, separate, her body tuned up, unsatisfied, for some explanation.

Eventually, he said, 'I'm sorry. I just couldn't get — going.' He sounded puzzled. 'Actually I'm bushed. I think I should get some sleep.' He turned and patted her thigh. 'Goodnight.'

'Please don't.' The pressure of her breasts against his back was unbearable. Her pubic hair felt like a lively spider. Her hands still trickled over his body. 'Please don't.' Her tongue dug against his ear, wetly. He thought he was going to be sick and hung over the side of the bed. The spasm passed. 'I'm sorry. It's just it's first thing. I haven't woken up yet.' He grabbed his cigarettes and shoved one between his lips. Thank God the matches were on the other side of the room.

Christine, in her rush to get to bed with him before he fell asleep, had left her clothes scattered by the bath. He was shaving and thinking how unpleasant his eyes looked, pouchy and selfish, when, in the mirror, he caught sight of something white, frilly and spattered with blood. Badly shaken, he turned and dropped the razor.

'What's this?' he shouted.

She appeared in the doorway and, following the direction he was looking in, saw her knickers. 'Oh, I'm sorry,' she said lightly.

'For Crissake!'

She gathered up her clothes.

'Clean it up!' he shouted.

She looked at him, angrily. 'All right, Ken. Since when have you been so fastidious?'

'It gave me a shock.' He sounded weak and unattractive.

'Pitiful.' She picked up his razor and held it out to him. Suddenly he did not want to touch it. She put it on the shelf by the mirror and said, 'It's the coil. I always bleed heavily at the beginning. It—'

'Well, do something else. Get on the pill.' He flung on his jacket and left. She tracked him down by the lift. 'I can't stand it.'

'What?'

'The blood. Your periods are too much for me.'

'Well . . . thank you.'

'They'd be too much for anyone.'

It was his birthday, and cards and flowers filled the flat. She sat on the couch, one shapely leg drawn up, painting her toe-nails. She was so disturbed her finger-nails were smudged and her eyebrows would have to be done again. Her new clothes were spread across the living-room; and looking at the yellows, the blacks, the scarlet suit, gave her some satisfaction. She looked again at one of his cards, a slim wispy blond with a pale face. Gordon, his assistant, had sent it. Why?

The phone rang. 'Wendy! Marvellous! Everything's fantastic! He's been offered so many commercials. I've just spent nearly 200 quid on new gear. You should see it . . .' The sadder she became, the louder she got. Her voice sounded quite jolly.

He came in surprisingly early, dressed in a new suit; its colour only emphasised his tiredness and pallor. He threw down an unwrapped present, lit a cigarette and stood in the middle of the living-room as though he was on a visit and none of this belonged to him.

'Must go, Wendy! Bye.' She put down the receiver and the phone instantly started to ring again.

'Sod it!' he said angrily. 'Don't answer it!'

They waited for it to stop. Finally he scooped it up. 'Yes?' Bunty wanted him to go gambling.

'I can't. I'm going out to dinner with my wife.'

Her laughter pealed into the living room. 'What are you doing that for?'

'It's my birthday. And tell Joel not to send our monthly quota of Snap. I do not want it.'

He'd write lies about it, give it a title, set it to music — but he wouldn't let his dog eat it.

7

Before Snap, they had spent their evenings together. Whatever they had done during the day, it was an unspoken rule that they would be in the flat around six; she would open a bottle of wine, he would play with Matthew, and her girlfriends would stay off the phone. Her girlfriends said that domestic life did not suit Ken: Christine had bitten off more than she could chew, he overlapped her at every point, it was only a matter of time before he left her. They didn't take into account the fact that he needed her strength and loyalty — that he was excited and encouraged by her lack of inhibitions in bed, that he was fed up with dry clever girls always challenging his intellect.

Her idle chatter soothed him. It went on around him, making no demands, leaving him free to think about something else or not to think about anything at all. She gave him well-cooked food, well-pressed clothes, and comfort, into which he could sink without question. For a long time he was very grateful to Christine.

After Snap, a pop group wanted him to arrange music, Joel wanted him to add class to his dinner parties, the agency wanted him for more ads, and Bunty wanted him.

One night he stayed in. Christine had made a curry and they sat on the floor watching television. Since he'd started being absent after six, Christine's girl-friends, like vultures, swooped in, and the phone rang incessantly. 'Wendy! Sorry. Phone you tomorrow.'

He flicked his plate to one side, his face expressionless. The shutters were down.

'Pat! I'll call you back.'

He plunged his hands into his pockets.

'Sorry, Ken. Would you like some coffee?'

He didn't answer, and she got up and opened the window. It was spring

101

She was standing near him and he could smell her perfume. He looked round, his eyes level with her full calves. They were packed with flesh like ripe pears. Beneath them her legs tapered dramatically into the slender ankles she was so fond of. Suddenly they were ludicrous, vulnerable, these two pieces of leg that filled his vision. He didn't like the way they were covered with frail black stocking as though to tempt, to invite. He couldn't see them belonging to a body. He preferred them lying twisted, shoeless, the black stocking torn and laddered. The top of the legs—raw flesh, orange and scarlet, globular flesh dripping with blood, arteries cut loose and dangling, smelling like old beef steak.

He turned and stared at the television, shaking and pale.

Her perfume suddenly stank—it filled the room, cheap and stale.

Christine could not remember his being so quiet. Suddenly she was very unsure of herself and couldn't think of a thing to say. She poured his coffee, pushed it across to him and sat down. Sighing, he turned off the set.

What could she talk about? She looked round desperately for something. The cat? The carpet? The programme he'd just switched off? She couldn't think of a thing that wouldn't sound silly and inconsequential. She continued silent.

After some minutes he turned and said, ferociously, 'What's the matter with you?'

'Nothing. I feel quiet.' She felt she should justify it. 'I don't know why. Perhaps it's the—' He was going further and further away from her and she couldn't think of a thing to draw him back—'I went to look at—' The sentence didn't deserve finishing. Feeling stupid, inadequate, she decided that talking about him might be the answer. His replies were short and gave her no encouragement.

Christine's talents, silent ones, expressed themselves best in the bedroom, and she and Ken spent most of the time so occupied. Her art as a conversationalist had seen little action, and now, put to the test, was found to be poor.

10 p.m. It was well past the hour when he'd reach for her hand, kiss her, take her to bed.

'I saw some denim suits round the corner, Ken. Fantastic.

102

Really good, on the shoulder. You'd look fantastic in one.'

'How much?'

'Only eight. Fantastic.'

'I'll look at them tomorrow.'

Silence.

'The pale ones have —'

'Oh do shut up about it!' He lit another cigarette.

Stung, she wanted to get up and leave the room, but she couldn't even manage that. She wanted to say, 'What's wrong? Why don't you want to make love to me? Is it me?' She was reminded of the time she first saw him. He seemed as unknown but unlike then there were no flashes of interest, excitement. Nothing about him was familiar.

'What's wrong?' Fatal.

'It's the bloody phone,' he shouted. 'It never stops. I have to get away from it.'

'Shall I take it off the hook?' As though in protest, it rang; and she answered it quickly. 'For you, darling.' She'd recognised Bunty's voice and made plenty of the endearment.

Bunty said, 'I've hung a moon among the stars.'

'Christ!' He wiped a hand over his face and remembered that this was his employer's wife. 'How d'you mean?' in a softer tone.

'In the studio of course. It's a hanging moon and lights up. It's also a zodiac moon and shows the influence of the planets. Mars into Jupiter and all that. You do believe in that. Well, if not you're a rarity.'

'Oh Christ!'

'Joel had a marvellous idea. He wants the magician for his cornflakes ad. He was quite cute about your knife, wasn't he? I'm glad you like the new amplifier. I insisted Joel got it. Anything else you need?' She laughed, and the laugh was nice and made him feel a bit better. 'There's a Hollywood producer in town. He does musicals and I've told him how great you are. I'm going to give a dinner for you. I'll invite him. There's a banker I want you to meet. We'll have a couple of filmstars, just for colour. If you need me for anything just call. Let the phone ring for some time because if the girl's out and my machine's on I can't hear it.'

'What machine?'

'What?' she laughed.

He sighed and said, patiently, 'You said something about a machine.'

'I didn't.'

Nasty, crawling panic, starting in his stomach. His mouth was dry.

Bunty said, 'It removes hairs, permanently. I spent four hours doing it last night. One leg's nearly done. The hairs have gone from my wrists, so have those from my nipples.'

Horrified, he said, 'You've hairs there?'

She laughed. 'Ken, what are you talking about?'

'The hairs around your nipples.'

There was a pause. 'Goodness me!' She sounded shocked. 'You must be drunk.'

Frightened, he put the phone down. Quite clearly he'd heard her talk about unwanted hair. Suddenly he was sure her teeth were false. That's why her S's whistled. Sickened, he turned to the television.

Christine poured more coffee. 10.30. Half an hour to go and then he could reasonably shut himself up in the dark. Christine's heavy hair fell forward on to her thighs—black, sleek, catching the light. It was dangerous. He had to look away, but even with his eyes on the ad break he couldn't get it out of his mind. It seemed to stroke her glistening thighs. It suggested many possibilities. He stood up. 'I think I'll go to bed and read something.' He didn't like the way her breasts divided. He wished she could be covered up, all of her.

Christine changed into her gold pyjamas and put on a Stones LP: she moved sensuously.

'I've got to go.'

'What?' She turned off the hi-fi.

'I've just remembered something at the studio. I won't be long.'

'What?'

'Gordon's cough-mixture-45-seconds.'

She watched from the window. He didn't go near the Porsche but walked quickly towards the station.

He walked for a long time and when he got into some anonymous narrow streets he felt curiously relieved. He liked the tightness, the dark, the uneven pavements. He liked particularly the smell of a box of rubbish bulging and swollen in the gutter. He went from doorway to doorway, staying in each a few moments, waiting. There were few people about. It was what he wanted, almost.

Soft flesh, quivering buttocks, plump thighs, perfumed hair — it had all been so attractive. Now it filled him with nausea and, strangely, fear. Not all the time. It seemed to catch him at unguarded moments. It wasn't that he found the women ugly — it was something about their flesh, their mouths . . . he couldn't describe it, except to say it gave him a funny feeling.

Christine's mammoth body, starved of love, took to indecent posturing. He'd find her lying on the black leather couch looking like something from a porn magazine. Gone were the gold tin-foil pyjamas and in their place, spicy underwear. She seemed unable to sit in a chair without turning it into some erotic pose, but the only spasm she provoked in him was the involuntary one of nausea. He started to avoid her. He took every job offered him and worked far into the night. Coming home, he'd often be drawn to the narrow streets. They were never satisfactory.

Bunty's pink rounded cheeks and lovely, easy smile, which he'd been so enthusiastic about, no longer moved him. He saw only long pink-brown nipples poking through tufts of hair, and false teeth. He couldn't get false teeth out of his mind.

He wondered if he was turning queer, and as they worked in the studio he'd catch sight of Gordon's tiny, well-shaped arse; but it did nothing for him, nothing at all.

8

Ken sat, not at the head of the table as he'd expected — seeing
that Bunty had said that the dinner was for him — but on one
side between a Greek boy who was trying to get money together
to make feature films and a middle-aged woman with an
unlikely name. She said she was a theatrical agent. After
several glasses of the rather bad wine, she said her speciality
was girls for skin flicks. The Hollywood musical producer
didn't seem to be there. There were two bankers, but they were
up at the end near the film star, who was getting all the
attention, even Bunty's. At the other end sat a politician, and
the least dim-witted guests, it seemed, were placed around
him. Ken was furious. This had never happened to him in his
life. He'd get through the main course and go.

Opposite him sat a short fat man in the same toad class as
Joel. His washed-out face was vaguely recognisable. He had a
New York accent and sensational hay-fever. His eyes were
inconsolable.

He leaned towards Ken. 'You know it's unusual to see
someone use right and left to cut with.'

'Yes,' said Ken shortly. He might be ignored, but things
could be worse.

'I suppose you were born like it?'

'What are you talking about?'

'I'm remarking on your ambidextrousness. I don't know the
correct term. I'm sure you do.'

'Ambidexterity.' Then it occurred to Ken that the pale toad
was trying to pick him up. 'I can assure you it does not apply to
me. I am right-handed.'

'But I've been watching you.'

The table was suddenly quiet.

'I've seen you cut your steak with your left hand, then your
right.'

'For Godsake!' Ken shouted. 'Allow me the benefit of the doubt about my own habits.'

'I wouldn't have thought he was ambidextrous,' Bunty cut in. 'Not at all.'

'I am not!' Ken said angrily.

The agent said, 'Methinks he doth protest too much.'

A woman squealed with laughter. Ken's eyes flashed. The film star said, 'It must come in quite handy.' Loud laughter.

Bunty leaned over as she poured the brandy and her enormous breasts almost fell out of the dress. She giggled and held them in.

'Are you a friend of Joel's as well?' asked the Greek.

'Yes,' Ken snapped and lit a cigarette.

'I hoped he'd be here tonight. I want to meet him.'

'He's in New York.' Ken turned to the skin-flick specialist.

'You're obviously not in the trade,' she told him.

'Why?'

'The way you insulted fatty opposite. Don't you know who is?' She murmured some name Ken thought he'd heard of. 'He's the gossip columnist for all the movie mags. He makes and breaks.'

'Well, he won't get the chance with me. I'm in advertising.'

The pale toad was buried deep in a new bunch of tissues. Then Bunty moved the vase of flowers and things seemed to improve.

'There's a big deal going on at the top of the table,' Bunty whispered as she poured Ken's brandy. Her soft hair brushed his face. 'There's going to be something good in it for you,' and this was the only reference she made, the whole evening, to his reason for being there. 'Trust me.' Her free hand, out of sight of the guests, stroked his back. 'You haven't drunk your wine.'

'It's vile.' He looked again at the bottle and wondered what Mouton Cadet had done to their vineyards since he'd last had it.

'Oh no! D'you think anyone else notices?' She breathed into his ear. 'I keep all the empty bottles with good labels and fill them with double litres of cheap stuff from the supermarket. I save pounds. Don't tell Joel.' She moved on.

Marooned among half-failures and nonentities, he watched the action at the ends of the table. The politician and the star attracted hangers-on like magnets, and they formed defensive groups and survived, even on the wine. The rest sat waiting for what had been privately promised. Bunty swayed round with the brandy and the black chocolates and whispered a 'Trust me' here and a 'It's all happening for you' there. Her cornflower-blue eyes were innocent.

'Bunty is very kind,' said the Greek. 'She is going to do a lot for me. When she smiles it's like the sun coming out in a dark sky.'

Ken swallowed his brandy.

'Are you gay?' asked the skin-flick agent.

'No I am not,' he replied promptly.

'Don't mind my asking. I'm a dyke.'

He looked at her acid hair, dyed and curled almost out of existence — it had the sugary impermanence of candy floss — at her silver satin suit clamped to her flat chest like armour, at her wrinkles and bags held at bay — just. Neither she, nor her statement interested him in the least. Ken and his two neighbours formed a silent peninsular jutting conspicuously out of the gaiety all around.

'Would you change places with me?' he said to her. 'The Greek man next to me would love to talk to you and I'd like to say something to the man at the end of the table.' He also wanted to get away from those sneering pale eyes opposite.

They changed places. He leaned across diagonally, forced himself into the conversation and became another of the politician's hangers-on.

It was after midnight and the guests were still around the table. The politician hadn't known Ken's name or anything about him. Ken had corrected this. He'd handled politics deftly; he'd hinted at his mother, he'd moved up next to the politician; he'd been invited to his home the following Sunday. Ken felt much better. The agent and the Greek film-maker sat silent. They hadn't been rescued.

It was just before people started going home that it happened. Bunny sat on the politician's knee, her bosom and legs looking safe, almost desirable. Ken had forgotten her dentures, her hairyness; and she was saying, 'It's nice to have everyone still at the table. Very French.' Ken turned round for no reason and saw a young, pretty girl lean across the table and bite the skin-flick agent in the arm.

108

He thought it was a game until he saw the teeth, large and square, as they crunched into the thin upper arm. The agent, rigid with pain, tried to push the girl's head away. She pulled her hair, tore at her cheeks. The teeth clung on. Blood appeared, the invincible crimson army, slowly at first, like sunrise, then rushing, splashing down the arm, on to the girl's face. Nobody took any notice.

Ken jumped up. His glass tipped over. 'For Crissake!' People took no notice of him as he dashed from the room.

He couldn't get to the lavatory in time. He was sick in the cat litter tray.

9

'Why did you go like that?' Bunty's voice was cold. He didn't answer, didn't want to speak to her. 'It comes to something when I, the hostess, have to ring you for an apology.' There was a pause, but if she was waiting for an apology she didn't get it. 'I've done a lot for you. So has Joel. Joel's put everything your way. Never mind about me. What a way to treat him. I know he wasn't there; but it is his house, his food and his bloody wine. It'll get back to him. You're just a snob!' she shouted. 'Just because my guests aren't quite up to what you think you're used to.'

'Your evening was a mess.' His voice, though soft, was effective. 'I have never been to such an incongruous dinner party in my life. No one knew anyone. No one was introduced. No one, not even a good hostess, would put those people together. They could never mix, except perhaps in some national emergency.'

Long peals of laughter. 'Oh Ken.'

'I didn't expect to have to sit through that mess to be ignored.' Her amusement was not catching.

'Of course you weren't ignored. Everyone loved you.' She was still laughing.

'I do not like being ignored; but more, I do not like people who behave in that way.'

She stopped laughing.

'Nobody helped her.'

'I think there's something I missed, Ken.'

'The young innocent-looking girl—'

'The banker's girl-friend—'

'Leaned right across the table and bit the blond agent in the arm—and I don't think it was a hint she was hungry.'

'I wish I'd seen it. She's a dyke, the agent. Probably been touching the girl up under the table.'

110

'It wasn't like that. The woman was howling with pain. Blood shot out. It splashed . . .'

Bunty waited for him to continue, then murmured, 'Incredible.'

'And people didn't do anything.'

'Perhaps they thought the women were just playing around. You know—kissing and stuff. The agent was very drunk. Anyway, why didn't you do something about it?'

'Because it was disgusting.' he said quickly. 'I've never seen people behave like that. I had to leave.'

'Prig! Anyway I've heard of some excuses. If it did happen—'

'If!'

'It wouldn't matter. So what!' And Bunty remembered the agent leaving. She remembered especially her arms, the way they pushed lightly into the fur sleeves. 'You know bloody well you're just making excuses for your rotten behaviour.' She smashed down the phone.

Christine came into the bedroom and seeing him still lying down decided to take advantage of it. She threw off her clothes. 'You know, darling, Matt just said Weetabix.'

Christine started using the same responses for all phone calls. 'Happy' became 'ecstatic'. 'Fantastic' and 'incredible' became 'out of this world'. Her voice, edgy with panic, had risen unattractively. It could never have passed for excitement if every other sentence didn't stress how excited she was. She brain-washed her girl-friends. She had no one to talk to.

She decided it could not go on when she got into bed with him only to have him leap out the other side and put his clothes on even faster than she'd taken hers off.

'What's wrong, Ken?'

'What's wrong? What's wrong? Nothing's wrong.'

'You behave very oddly.'

'Who wouldn't with a sex maniac pawing him all the time?'

She pushed her head into the pillow and didn't hear him leave. The phone seemed more insistent than ever as she lay, crushed, and Wendy, Pat and Lilly, deprived of her, kept ringing. She caught it during the few minutes it was free and called Frances.

'I thought we might go shopping again,' she said quickly,

Agitation would have to do for excitement. 'It was a wonderful day, wasn't it?'

'Yes.'

She waited for Frances to mention his running away. When she didn't, Christine said, 'I can't stand it.'

'What did you say?'

'His running away. Don't you think running away like that was odd? I mean, what do you think?'

'Yes, it was odd. Success does funny things to people.'

'Success? That's the last thing I'd have thought of. It's not as though he'd be recognised, although that's just how he looked before he ran. Did someone see him?'

'I wonder!'

'Perhaps he thinks he should behave oddly to go with the image. Is that what you mean?'

'I think he can't take success. He's guilty about succeeding.'

'Frances, you are so clever. You really are.'

'He's in conflict.'

'What will happen?'

'He'll either learn to cope with being successful or start failing. He'll do something—his subconscious will. It occurred to me he might crash the car.'

'Oh no.' Christine was so alarmed she lit the cigarette the wrong end and choked. 'What's the dog-food woman like?'

Christine mistook her silence, but Frances was just finding it hard to describe Bunty.

'It doesn't matter, Frances. I know he fancies her.'

'No. I don't think she's got anything to do with it. She's silly and rural.'

Christine sighed. 'Suddenly it's all gone. I sat naked in front of the mirror. I'd just washed my hair and I asked him to come and brush it. He wouldn't. He always used to. I love having my hair brushed.'

'It does happen, Christine, especially after a couple of years.'

Christine searched desperately for some piece of optimism.

'His track record isn't encouraging,' Frances admitted.

'He said he left the others because he didn't love them.'

'Found he didn't love them. Anyway, he's got a child this time.'

Christine hoovered the green carpet, polished the couch, took a few minutes off for her bending and stretching twenty. She phoned the studio and he said he would come home for dinner. She spent the afternoon cooking, massaged her face, found she was too fat for her new scarlet suit, and opened some wine.

He didn't come home.

At nine o'clock the studio rang to say he'd run into a problem with cough-mixture 40-seconds and he'd gone to the agency. He wouldn't be long.

At ten o'clock she phoned Frances. At eleven o'clock she started drinking.

Frances said there was nothing she could do except wait. 'Be calm. Do something. Read — I mean — ' She glided over that delicate area. 'He won't be long.'

'I'm not a saint. And I'm hungry. The dinner's ruined. By the way, Gordon sent him a birthday card of a slim curly-haired blond. Does it mean anything?'

'Perhaps Gordon thought thin, delicate blonds are Ken's ideal type,' she laughed.

Stunned, Christine threw away the dinner, locked the food cupboard and changed her life.

10

Christine lost seven pounds in one week and had her hair cut short and curled in one morning. She didn't feel quite ready for the final bleached step yet. She put away her bright make-up and started using pale pinks, soft greys, a touch of blue. She polished her nails with an old-fashioned buffer and paste and coated her dark skin with ivory cream. She didn't quite look like the girl on the card, but she was getting there. Ken thought it was nice for people to have a change.

Ken treated Joel as though he was highly intelligent, and Joel liked it, although he hardly understood a thing Ken was saying. He loved it when Ken pointed out the crassness and stupidity of other people.

He was sending Ken to Paris to supervise French Snap. First-class travel, best hotels and, afterwards, a holiday anywhere in Europe at his expense.

Bunty phoned, 'When are you going to Paris?'

'Next month.'

'I might drop over for a few days.'

He felt uneasy. 'That'll be nice for you,' he managed to say. 'Bring Joel.'

'I've told him to send you first-class and afterwards a holiday.'

He nodded. The studio was hot and he couldn't quite reach the window.

'Well,' she said. 'You have a funny way of saying thankyou.'

'Sorry—I don't feel myself . . .'

'Are you always so enthusiastic about what's offered you?'

He thought about the big loose plates of teeth and shuddered.

'Perhaps you're frightened,' she said.

The studio was getting very hot. It felt like late summer. For a moment he couldn't remember what month it was. He took off his jacket. No longer sure what she was saying, he exclaimed, 'At the moment I like things out of reach, yes. I'm sorry, Bunty. I'm so busy I can only tolerate the most superficial scenes with anybody.'

He hung up and tried to open the window. April 20. The studio, even hotter, smelt disturbingly of beer and fried fish and there was a stink of horse shit. Outside, shouting, laughing, rather drunken. There were a lot of people suddenly. Carts were passing, he could hear wooden wheels. They were fast for carts and he started towards the window and heard a child cry, *'Watercresses.'*

Then the phone rang.

Bunty said, *'Don't be frightened of fatboy.'*

'Who's fatboy?'

The line went dead.

He was sitting on the high stool with the ear-phones on, balancing a jingle, when she came in. She wore a blue silk dress, which brought out the colour of her eyes. Her hair had just been done in another regal style, and she was looking, as Joel would say, 'like a lot of class,' and she knew it.

'What do you want?' His eyes were slaty and disapproving.

'I just phoned you.' She pretended to be cross. 'You don't take any notice of anything I say. I told you I've got you a present.'

His heart sank. Did she mean the present of her body?

She dipped into the carrier bag and brought out two small plants in pots. 'Tomato plants. You've got a conservatory. You can grow things. It'll be good for you to get green-fingers. Calm you down.'

'That's very kind of you, Bunty.' He fingered the crisp leaves.

'You work far too much, you know. Gordon said you're here all night sometimes. Ease up, Ken. You're all right.' She wanted to touch him but the way he was looking discouraged that move. She took out her compact and looked at her perfect skin. 'You don't like jingles do you?'

'No I do not like bloody jingles. I'll do French Snap and that's it.'

'What about writing music for a feature film?' she said

smoothly, touching on at least half of his cherished ambitions.

After a thoughtful pause, he nodded. He believed she could get him what he wanted, but he didn't know if he could trust her.

'Well, let's get you fixed up with that,' she was saying. 'Come back to my place and we'll talk about it.'

'I've got twenty minutes to finish this. You're welcome to stay here — or, better still, why don't you pop over to the pub and have a drink?'

'What pub?'

He indicated the window. 'Opposite.'

She pulled a face at him. 'Since when do they serve liquor in an office block?'

He gasped, then tried to laugh. 'I was joking.' He was sure he'd smelt beer.

'You behave yourself. Don't start rushing off making excuses about lady cannibals. Actually it's very original.'

'You bitch!'

'Oh come on, Ken. I phoned both of them. We had a good laugh.'

For a moment, as much as she liked him, there was something — a spark, an expression in his eyes. She was afraid. Then it was gone.

'You are a funny man.' She tried to laugh. 'I can't make you out. Still, I suppose that's why you're so attractive.'

'I love Christine,' he said and turned back to his work.

When she'd lost a stone and a half and he still didn't show any sign of excitement, Christine decided to have a serious talk. She hardly ever saw him. Then when he did appear, one evening, early, the flat was full of girls. She was giving away her fat clothes and her girl-friends were picking, pecking at them like birds. Her back to the window, Christine stood wearing a new slim, belted suit with wide trousers.

'What's Ken's new assistant like?' asked one of the girls.

'I don't know.'

'Don't you see him when you go to the studio?' asked Wendy.

'Oh I don't go there,' Christine said airily. 'I never go near it', as though it was her choice rather than his. 'Let Pat have the blue skirt. It suits her.'

116

'With a dishy old man like yours I'd be there all the time.'

'You'll have to shorten that dress and take it in.' Christine pounced on the loose material and gathered it in at the waist. 'Out of this world, isn't it? You shouldn't wear false eye-lashes. Not a whole lid full like that. Cut four or five off the strip and stick them in with your own. More natural.'

'Is it true he spends all night at the studio?' said Wendy.

'He's incredibly busy. Gets about an hour's sleep. I don't know how he does it.'

'I heard he's on Speed,' said Pat.

'I wouldn't be surprised.' Christine laughed.

'I saw him the other day,' Pat continued.

'Oh yes. Where?'

'Near St Pancras Station. It was late, after midnight. I didn't think it was him at first because he was walking.'

'You're very quiet today, Christine,' said Wendy.

'She is, isn't she?'

'It's the slimming,' said Lilly. 'Make sure you take vitamins and plenty of liquid.'

'I suppose he was with Frances when you saw him by the station?' Christine said quietly.

'No. He was on his own.'

'You must find it hard cooking for him,' said Lilly.

'He's hardly here,' she admitted and regretted it immediately. 'I mean he's got such a social life. He's so "in". The phone never stops. He met the Prime Minister the other night. He's off to Paris in two weeks. Something very big.'

'Why doesn't he take you?' asked Wendy.

Silence. He was in the room.

Seeing the flock of long-legged, half-naked girls wading in the swirling mass of bright clothes, he laughed and said, 'Christ, a boutique. That's all I need.'

The girls covered up their bodies. One of them started talking about her cystitis.

'Get treatment,' said Wendy. 'If it goes to your kidneys it's serious.'

'I get a pain here.' The girl pressed the middle of her back. 'Is that your kidneys?'

'I don't know. I'm not sure where they are.'

117

'They're here.' Christine pointed to two places low in her hips.

'Higher,' said Ken. 'They're here behind the abdominal viscera, one on each side. They're surrounded by a lot of fat. They're bean shaped — reddish brown —'

'Fancy that!' said Wendy. 'Isn't your old man clever?'

'Since when have you been into anatomy?' asked Christine.

He didn't know what to say.

Wendy said, 'I don't know where my kidneys are — my liver, my ovaries. I just about know where my fanny is —'

'O.K., babes,' said Christine. 'Don't think I'm throwing you out . . .'

Armed with the colourful outsize treasures, they swooped away.

He fell asleep after dinner, so she couldn't have her serious talk. She sat, watching him sleep. She loved his wide nostrils, his straight nose; she loved him. She thought it funny after the numbers of men she'd had, three a night on occasion, coming in windows, down chimneys, that she should get so stuck on one and be so unhappy.

He smiled when he woke and stretched, and she thought he was going to get hold of her, but he was reaching for his cigarettes. As he moved she saw the erection. She trembled with all the pent-up desire, the deprivation. Her cheeks were hot.

He lit a cigarette and lay back looking at the ceiling. 'What time is it? How long have I been asleep?'

'Fantastic,' she breathed. 'You can get one in your sleep but you can't get one for me.'

His eyes flicked sideways. They were cold. 'If often happens when I wake up. It doesn't mean anything. Don't be so demanding all the time.' He gave her another wintry look and turned round.

'What is happening to us?'

'You're so clinging. It's unbelievable.'

Seeing her unhappy face made him swing his feet to the floor and stand up. Guilt, on top of everything else could be too much.

The she said, 'Is there someone else?' Perhaps it would all

118

come out in justified rage.

'No there is fucking not! But there will be if you keep on like this.' He kicked the brass table.

'What's the dog-food woman like? Beautiful?'

'She's not fucked up by sophistication.'

'You keep her out of sight.'

'I keep *you* out of sight. You're so thick.'

She recoiled, as though struck. 'You're destructive, Ken.'

'Who wouldn't be disturbed?' He'd misheard her. 'What person wouldn't be disturbed with someone prying into their every move! Don't tell me I'm disturbed. I can't even fall asleep without being accused of having a mistress. Be self-sufficient for Crissake. Learn to be responsible for yourself.' He put on his jacket.

Tears splashed down her face as he put his cigarettes and keys in his pocket. 'Where are you going?'

'For a walk. Some air.'

He went to the most unlikely place for air. He turned swiftly into the narrow streets by the railway line. The streets didn't smell right. He sniffed into doorways like a dog. They were all rinsed out of smell. He was furious.

Christine followed him.

He woke up. Someone was holding him. 'Why is it dark?' he asked. It shouldn't be dark. He'd been standing by a lighted stone stairway and the woman had been wearing lots of long skirts and petticoats. He remembered the feel of them clearly, how heavy they had been. He must be back in the alley again and he started shaking.

'It's all right. It's all right.' Christine rocked him gently.

'Where am I?'

'You're in bed. You've had a bad dream.' She spoke patiently, as though to a child.

'Put the light on.'

Held tight against her, he felt comfortable, safe, and didn't want to move, even for a cigarette. 'You're a good person, Christine.' He put his arms around her. Then he felt frightened. He mustn't get aroused, out of control. The glimpses he'd had once or twice when the flesh had looked funny made him scared to go near her.

119

He closed his eyes, wanted to sleep. 'I do love you, Christine.'
Then he remembered the woman with the petticoats.

Ken asked Frances to get him some iron tablets.

'If you feel run down, why don't you go to the doctor?' she
suggested.

'I never go near those people. I just want a pick-up. Get
vitamins as well. Yeast or whatever it is.'

'Being run down could be a symptom of something else. It's
not a good idea to treat yourself.'

'Frances,' he laughed. 'Please don't get deep with me about
medicine. I've had it all my life from my mother. Can't I just
ask for a simple thing and get it?'

She took the money and he watched her walk to the door.
She was wearing a long skirt. 'Frances.'

She turned round.

'Do women wear petticoats?'

'Only old women. If you're thinking of getting one for
Christine, forget it.'

'Long petticoats, I mean.'

She laughed. 'Of course not.' She opened the door.

'Well, when did they?' he asked sharply. The petticoats had
been very real. One of them was patched and rather dirty and
her skin smelt strongly of scented soap.

'Victorian times.'

'I'm being very good.' Christine, the front of her curly hair
dappled blond, ran her hands over her slim hips. 'I only had
two boiled eggs and three cups of black coffee yesterday. I'm
nine stone. Isn't it incredible?'

'Very good,' said Frances.

'Look at this.' She brought out a long box from under the
bed. 'Cost every penny I've got but it's worth it. A massaging
machine. It won't undo what's already done, but it stops any
more happening. I think flesh has to be exercised to be firm. I
think he'd go mad if I started to sag.'

'You look all right, Christine,' said Frances, only half
laughing. Christine's physical problems were non-existent
compared with her own.

They sat silently for some time.

120

'He's a very odd man,' Christine said. 'One minute he's leaving me, the next says he loves me. I think he's schizo.'

'He works too hard.'

'To get away from me, I expect. He's bored when he's here.'

'I'm sorry.'

'Actually he won't go near me.' She picked at the white bed-cover. 'I mean in the beginning we were at it all the time. He'd come back in his lunch hour and we'd do it. It was marvellous.'

'Love affairs do change, Christine.' Her voice was re-assuring. 'They're passionate to begin with. Then they settle down. They have to; otherwise you'd be worn out.'

'I want it back. It's got to come back.'

'There are some things you can't recapture. I don't think he's dissatisfied with you. He just wants to be peaceful.'

'We used to do it on the floor, on chairs, in the lavatory. I'll get him back. I'll do anything.'

As Frances was going out Christine said quietly, keeping an eye on the neighbour's door, 'He really is peculiar. Not just about me. When he's alone he mutters, and he goes for walks at night, near Kings Cross. It's odd, because he sort of flits along. One minute he's there, then I've lost him.'

'I know what you mean. We were standing in a crowd the other day and he disappeared. Bunty was furious. One minute he was there, the next he'd gone.'

11

When he got home she'd gone blond, but what really shocked him was the sight of a tin of slimming Snap being opened.

'You're not thinking of giving that to the dog?'

'I can still just about afford human slimming foods, thank you.' She picked up the china dish with DOG painted on the front. 'Your mother rang, or should I say rang off. She only has to hear my voice.'

'But I've forbidden Snap in this house.'

'Well, it hasn't got through to Mr Dogfood. He's just sent a box of thirty assorted tins. It's not going to waste. It sweeps the country, yet your pooch can't have it.'

'Dog!'

'Pooch!'

'Fucking dog!'

'Pooch!' she screamed and turning, wrenched her hand across the jagged tin.

Blood welled up and spilled on to the floor. She moaned with pain. He just stared, his face dry, paper-white.

'Christ, oh Christ, what have I done? I'm cut to the bone.' She staggered to the sink and turned on the cold tap. Matthew jumped up and down, screaming. 'It's all right darling,' she managed to say, as she lifted the gashed hand into the water.

Then he moved. He went to the phone.

'What are you doing?' she asked.

'Getting an ambulance.'

'Oh don't be daft.' She washed the cut without looking at it. The sight of the inside of her flesh as the cut flapped open made her feel queasy. 'Put the phone down, Ken,' she said firmly. 'Bring me the brandy. Get some bandages from the bathroom.'

He ordered an ambulance and got the bandages but wouldn't come into the kitchen. Without looking he threw the roll in her direction.

'Squeamish prat!'

He looked out of the window. 'Oh, let it come quickly. Oh God, let it come quickly. Please God.'

She appeared in the doorway, her hand swathed in white gauze.

'Stay in there.' His voice trembled.

'It's only blood for heavensake,' and she walked past him, over to the shelf, and poured a brandy.

'If you did what I said, this wouldn't have happened.'

'I'll be all right.'

'I wish the ambulance would hurry.'

'Are you serious? I'm not going to hospital in an ambulance. Cancel it, Ken. You'll look such a fool.'

'You are, Christine. You'll have to be — to be — You'll have to have —'

'Stitches.'

She was surprised he was so concerned and was quite cheered up by it. Her bandage grew red. He turned his back and pressed his head against the window. The glass was cool and drew out his heat, his panic. 'Go and lie down.'

'If you want me to go to hospital so much, drive me yourself.'

'No.' The scarlet, sopping bandage was beginning to drip. 'Go into the kitchen.'

'Why?'

'It's cleaner.'

The phone rang. He snapped it up and put it down ferociously. 'That games mistress, Jane.'

Then came the beautiful, safe, soothing sound of the ambulance siren.

In the hospital there was a complication. They stitched her hand, gave her a tetanus shot and sent her home.

'What are you doing?' he asked, as she came into the waiting room.

'Going home.'

He jumped up and without knocking went into the doctor's room.

'You must keep her in. That's a horrible cut. She's suffering from shock.'

123

'Your wife is perfectly all right. She certainly isn't shocked.'

Ken banged the desk. 'You're being irresponsible. You are not looking after her properly. I shall hold you responsible for the consequences.'

'What consequences?'

'Her—whatever happens to her.'

'I can't use national health beds for the wives of hypochondriacal husbands.' He hated Ken on sight.

'Then I'll pay. She's shocked. She's lost a lot of blood. She's had a lot of stitches. I want her looked after.'

Christine shared a two-bed cubicle with a woman who was still unconscious from an operation.

'What about Matthew?' she asked again.

'He'll be all right,' said Ken.

'I feel fine. This is ridiculous.'

'You won't. You'll get delayed shock.' He wiped a hand over his face. He was very tired. 'It's better not to take chances.'

She smiled. 'You are funny.' She'd never known him so solicitous.

He waited in the cubicle while she went to the lavatory. A nurse told him to put his cigarette out, so he bit his nails and wished he could go.

The woman in the next bed made a suggestion. He'd have found it slightly shocking coming from a prostitute in the street, leave alone from a patient recovering from an operation. Then he remembered that people coming round from anaesthetics were often obscene. He ignored her. She said it again. He went to the window.

Go on, let me. You'll like it. Her voice was unusually coarse and he turned and looked at her. She had a long narrow face on which beauty had collapsed into wrinkles and pouches. Her eyes glittered and her heavy make-up gave a suggestion of how she'd once looked. Her head was covered in tight woolly curls like a sheep's. *I won't charge you. I know how to do it, just how you like it. It's my speciality.* She coughed, a hacking cigarette cough.

He was used to women finding him attractive, but now he was entirely out of his depth. Christine would have to be moved. He could hear the sheets crackling as the woman

124

uncovered herself. *'Come on, pretty boy. Have a good look.'*

'Shut up, you hideous bitch!' He rushed out and down the passage.

'Nurse. Come quickly!'

'What is it?' the nurse asked calmly

'This woman — the one next to my wife.' He was breathless. Then he realised what had been so odd. It was unusual to see someone coming round from an operation wearing a theatrical make-up. 'She's saying some terrible things. I'd like my wife moved at once.'

The nurse started towards the cubicle, then stopped. 'She can't be round yet.'

'She is. She's fully conscious.'

The nurse pushed open the swing door. Ken followed. Christine was sitting in a chair. The woman was lying down again, the sheets and blankets almost covering her head and remarkably neat.

'She's fooling,' he assured the nurse.

'Mrs Lyons?' the nurse said cheerfully, and lifted back the sheet.

Ken saw a young girl, white-faced, deeply asleep.

'What was she saying?' asked the nurse and covered her again.

'Well . . .' He swallowed. 'She's . . .' Then he pulled himself together. 'She came round for a short time and went to sleep again.' He gave the nurse a brilliant smile.

'That's quite usual.'

He kissed Christine quickly and left her among the rustling uniforms and blue night-lights. She wasn't used to it. She didn't like it, but she was safe.

The nurse went into the office and said, scathingly, 'There's a vogue of this sort of thing in Hampstead. An epidemic of overshocked women. Remember that one we had last week. Cut herself shaving her armpit.'

'Oh, not another non-accident.'

12

'You wanted to get me out of the way.' For the first time since he's known her she was wearing a nightdress in bed. He could feel the stinging nylon next to his skin. 'It's obvious.' Sullen, resentful, she hadn't slept. 'I mistook your concern. I thought you were worried about me. You just wanted to be with her. That's why you shut me away.'

'I could hardly be with her, whoever she is. You rang me every ten minutes. Then you show up at dawn.' He looked at the big professional bandage lying on top of the coverlet. 'You shouldn't have discharged yourself.'

'The nurses understood. They thought it was mad I was there at all.'

He went back to sleep and when he woke it was mid-day. He was full of disgust—dull, satiated. His mouth tasted salty. He had a nasty, sharp twinge of panic. Then fingers started caressing his balls. 'Please stop!' He opened his eyes. Christine's lips were all over him. The muslin bandage was flapping in his face and her breasts wobbled as she went up and down on top of him. Whatever excitement she'd provoked in him asleep fizzled out immediately. Her full lips felt like a suction pump. He closed his eyes and tried to move his body with hers, to make some sense of the awful, desireless void. He used his hands skilfully, he kissed her energetically, he tangled with her short hair, he got on top of her.

'What's the matter?' Her voice was cool. She, an expert in the tactile truth of love, had not been fooled.

'I think I've been overdoing it at work.'

'Well, you certainly haven't here.' She gave a crazy laugh, then burst into tears.

The phone rang and Bunty said, 'Come and have a late breakfast or d'you want to go to the Hilton? I must see you. I've—'

He put the phone down.

His mother said, 'You're late.' She was curved over by the cake-stand and her black and yellow dress made her look like a ripe banana. 'Want something for your hangover?'

'I'm not hungover.'

'You look it.'

The phone rang and she said, 'It's for you.'

Sighing, he passed between the display of dead cakes and a Marino Marini sculpture.

Bunty said, 'I must see you.'

'For heavensake!'

'It's about the film.' She sounded offended.

'What about it?'

He felt a hand on his back and swung to one side. His mother said, 'Just taking a hair off your back. Blonds now?'

'The Hollywood producer's coming here in half an hour. Come and meet him.'

'All right.'

His mother poured him a black coffee. 'Would you like an Underberg Bitters? Soothes the hangover.'

'No thank you.'

'Dr Williams said I'm dying.'

'Oh do shut up.' His hair felt greasy. Next he'd be getting dandruff.

'I like your suit.'

'I got it in the Kings Road.'

'Are you going to put your child down for Eton?'

'Yes.'

'*She* won't like it.'

In profile she looked dangerous. Her nose dipped over her chin and her mouth disappeared. He supposed that that was what madness did to you. The mournful eye, the one he could see, was full of craftiness. He needed the other side of her face to balance her up, so he moved in front of her.

She leapt out of the chair with deadly speed and took hold of his tie. 'It's crooked.'

He froze.

At close range one or two whiskers hung almost to her chin. Her lemon skin, like a chameleon's, had changed to match the dress's pattern and was covered with dark-brown splodges of age like sunflowers. She patted his hair. 'Wanna talk about it?' Her lips touched his cheek.

The kiss stung him into action. He backed to the door. 'You used to be such a loving boy. Everyone said so.'

He had to keep her face full front. Then he felt all right. It was when he saw only bits of it that he felt shaky. 'Goodbye.'

He felt ill by the time he got to Bunty's and decided he should go and eat something; but the thought of meeting the producer excited him, so he lit another cigarette and rang the bell.

These days he not only noticed women's ugliness but seemed to attract it. Bunty's hair was straight and lank and hung in two plaits on either side of her face. She hadn't slept, and for some reason a double chin had appeared. This sudden decline was heightened by her surprising hair-style.

'Is he here?'

'No. Not yet. He must be held up. Is the traffic bad? D'you want a drink?'

'No thank you.'

She sat at the kitchen table and laughed at him.

'Where's he coming from?'

'The Dorchester. Excuse the way I look, but the girl walked out, so I've been cleaning the kitchen. I can't bear letting things go. You sure you don't want a scotch? Go on. Have a scotch.'

'I don't want one.' He sat opposite her and she looked into his eyes.

'Have a gin, then. Let yourself go.'

Suspiciously, he asked, 'What did this producer say exactly?'

'He'd like to meet you.'

Bunty wasn't exactly dressed to seduce him; so, feeling safer, he said, more politely, 'Has he heard the jingle?'

'Of course he has. Relax.'

He didn't believe her . . . the look in her eye. 'Did Joel play the whole tape?'

She nodded.

'Where is Joel?'

'Trying to trace that magician we saw.'

Ken sat, quiet, nervous. He kept running his fingers over his lips, and she no longer found it attractive. He looked at his watch.

'*It's all over with fat boy, if that's what you're worried about.*'

'I expect you have lots of affairs.' He sounded exhausted.

She arched her back like an angry cat. 'No I do not have affairs if it's any of your business. If you're trying to say you find me attractive, I'd rather you didn't sound so half-hearted.'

Confused, he muttered, 'Can't you ever talk about anything else?'

Softly, insiduously, '*D'you know how old Joel is? 82 at least. When I met him he was wrinkled as an alligator. He takes monkey hormones.*' In her usual voice, she added, 'I wasn't a nurse.' Softly: '*I just told him that. He was hung up on nurses' uniforms. He's disgusting.*'

'Leave him then, but don't keep going on about screwing.'

She frowned. They stared at each other.

'Ken,' she said slowly, 'Ease up a bit. I was only saying I wasn't really a nurse because I hadn't got my SRN . . .'

He sat, his eyes fixed on the table. He didn't know what she'd said, what she hadn't. He didn't dare think about it. He did know he'd heard it. He shuddered and held his hands pressed together between his knees. Suddenly he appealed to her. 'Oh Bunty, I feel terrible. Everything's terrible.'

'When I'm depressed I find it helps to go to bed.'

'Thank you but I don't think doing that would help at all,' he snapped. He was looking at his watch again. He no longer believed the film producer was coming, or that there was a film producer.

Suddenly he turned very white and she was about to ask what was the matter but he plunged out of the house, jumped into his car and left London . . .

He couldn't get out of his mind her naked breasts, white and full of tiny blue veins.

'*I've lost weight,*' she'd murmured. '*I look good naked now, but I always look good naked.*' She started to lift her sweater.

'No.'

She laughed. '*Don't you like it?*'

Everything was in a turmoil at the sight of that flesh and it wasn't pleasant. She was coming towards him. His head spun. 'No, damn you woman!' The blue veins throbbed, her breasts full of blood swung in front of him.

'But I'm crazy about you.'

'The dog woman is in London,' said Frances. 'What's more she doesn't know where he is. She said he was waiting at her house to meet a producer and he suddenly ran out for no reason. She's rather annoyed. She said she thinks he's working too hard.' Frances decided not to mention the loony sexual remarks that he'd made to Bunty.

Christine sat hunched in front of the mirror. She hadn't eaten or slept for days. Yet, if anything, she looked even more beautiful.

'Come on.' Frances pushed across the cup of consommé. 'You've got to keep your strength up. You've got Matthew, and he needs you.'

Listlessly she picked up the cup. The phone rang, and the way she grabbed for it showed that she hadn't altogether lost hope.

'Jane! Yes I was in hospital. Nothing much. I cut my hand. Ken made me go in. He's so protective. He's doing so well it's out of this world. He'll be on Russell Harty next.' She put the phone down and lay on the bed.

'I'd go out with someone, if I were you,' said Frances. 'You must still know some men.'

'I could have done a couple of years ago, but since I've been with him . . .' She put the soup down.

'I'm not talking about playing around. The attention, the loving will do you good. You need it. Then when he comes back you'll be in better shape.'

'I wonder if my past has put him off. I was stupid to tell him.'

'The soup's gone cold. Shall I heat it up?'

'I've been wondering if it's something I've done sexually. I get carried away. It could be so many things.'

In the end she decided it was her bosom. When he'd said, 'Lovely new breasts' to describe someone's daughter, he was obviously saying he liked them, so she scoured London looking for a pectoral water-massager.

130

After five days she started taking tranquillisers and had her hair dyed white. Her make-up became surrealistic. She looked like something from outer space.

At three a.m. she phoned Frances. 'I think I should get the police.'

'Take your pills.'

'I've had them, three times over. Hang on. There's a car.' Heart racing, she went to the window. Nothing. 'I've been through all his papers, note books, letters. It all looks so innocent. I'm sure that was him just now.'

'How much have you drunk?'

'I wish the night was over. I feel as though I'm in a submarine. There's no air in this flat.'

'You shouldn't drink with those pills.'

'The sodding birds'll start singing next.' She'd had at least two bottles of wine.

'I think you should do something to give you an anchor — a job, or take a course in something. Learn a language.'

'I suppose he's told you he resents keeping me and you're being tactful about it. Jingling stops him being creative.' She hiccoughed. 'Pardon me. Yes I'll get a job.' For a moment she was almost cheered up. Then she saw his hair-brush. 'I'll do anything if he'll come back. Anything. All I can think of is the good times, how beautiful it was, the joy. I can't get it out of my mind, and that's the most hurtful thing of all.'

She went into the kitchen, opened the refrigerator, knelt down and put her head in. 3.15 a.m. It was the only bearable place.

For six days he didn't do anything. He walked through grass, lay down, took his meals alone, slept, read the newspapers. The only person he spoke to, a seventeen-year-old girl, said, 'Adverts on telly? Do those things have music? I never noticed.'

Colour came back into his face; he felt calm. His life in London had broken his health. He hated his job. He loved the silence and smell of the country. He'd get Christine and Matthew, borrow money from his mother again and buy a farm just outside the village.

He sat outside the pub and drank the local draught beer. In

half an hour he'd have dinner—roast duck, new peas, half a bottle of Beaune. He watched a family go into the church. His mind was quiet and empty—safely empty—and he felt he could fill it with any subject and it would be all right. He moved his chair to catch the last of the sun—and then it happened, suddenly between one thought and the next. He jumped up and ran to his car. He had to get back to London. He had to get back into the smells and doorways of the narrow streets.

The police stopped him before he was half-way. 'You know you've been doing 80?'

'It's imperative I'm in London. It's a matter of life and death.'

They believed him.

She was sitting in front of her beauty products, looking in the mirror. He didn't notice the new bed-spread, the little plants on the window-sill or the repainted walls. She was stark with depression.

'Come on,' he said softly and patted her hair. 'Let's go for a drive.'

They went to Wheelers for an aperitif and had lunch at the White Tower. They got Matthew from nursery and drove to Brighton. They came back to London and went to a late-night film. For two days they whirled around the best places. They thought of going to Paris. Christine had never felt so unhappy.

He waited while she washed her hair.

'Aeroplane, Daddy.'

'No, Matthew, we're going by car. You'll see the Arc de Triomphe and the Champs Elysée.'

Then he saw her knickers.

He'd gone into the bedroom. He was so desperately tired he knew that if he lay down he'd be unconscious for hours, so he splashed his face with Cologne, and there, white and sinister, they lay twisted by the bed. Even their position was obscene. He stared, fascinated. Tart's knickers. He couldn't touch them or go near them and rushed out of the room.

'Christine! Clear up the bloody place. I can't stand clothes everywhere. I've got to live here too.'

She charged into the bedroom like a bull, her hair dripping

and soapy. 'Where? Where's the mess? Show me! One pair of clouts!'

She punched him, and her knuckles hurt his lip. He backed away; he didn't like violence. She moved towards him, her eyes scarlet. She was going to hit him again. He made an involuntary movement, and his body seemed to close in on itself, his hands covering as many of the vulnerable places as they could. She didn't hit him. Almost sneering, she turned her back, offering him an advantageous chance, and then shrugged her shoulders and went to the mirror.

'You wiggle like an air hostess. You're all wriggling and stupid.'

'Of course.' Her voice crackled with sarcasm. Even her hair seemed full of it; it snapped and cracked as she combed it. She lit a cigarette and flooded her eyes with blue eye-drops.

'You're synthetic. Boring.'

'Of course.'

'I can't stand women who don't do anything.'

'Incredible.'

'Don't keep using that fucking word. I am sick to death of your misuse of language.'

'Too, too incredible.' Then she murmured, 'Coward.'

He waved his arms. 'I happen to prefer tenderness.'

'There you go, turning your failings into virtues again. You make me more stupid than I am. Whatever faults anyone has, you make them worse.' She mascaraed her lashes, painted her lips. She didn't feel quite as cool as she saw him pick up his keys and cigarettes. 'Where are you going?'

'Back to the studio. Where else?'

13

The only good thing about the summer was the tomatoes. He loved the way they ripened; there was something solid about a large crimson tomato. He bought over a hundred plants and spent most of his spare time in the conservatory. He bought books about them and learned their Latin names, and people were surprised to hear this 'in' jingle-writer suddenly start talking about tomatoes and their habits.

Christine's perfect breasts were massaged and exercised, watered and pampered, and they thrived almost as well as his tomatoes. Everybody wanted her, except Ken. He felt he should want her. He did want something, but he didn't know what it was.

'Men follow me up the street. The *Sun* stopped me yesterday and asked if I'd pose nude. Ken would never allow it.' Then she remembered it was Frances she was talking to. 'Actually, he has gone prim. Keeps washing his hands. Can't bear anything even a touch risqué. Wendy told a joke the other day and he walked out. I never know what he's doing. If only he'd phone me and let me know. I was awake all night, because he said he'd ring—he promised he'd ring. He rang the next morning, worried about his dog. Did I get it fresh meat? For Godsake! The funny thing is, the dog doesn't like him any more. It skulks away when Ken comes in.'

Bunty came to the studio one afternoon while he was putting in new plants. 'I haven't seen you for ages.'

'I don't like being tricked,' he said.

'You weren't! The producer showed up that morning and you'd gone. He was furious, but I calmed him down. I played him Vic Damone records.'

He didn't believe her.

'Shall we go for a walk? I like walking.'

134

He looked at her glistening, lascivious lips and snarled, 'I bet you do.'

'Is this what you want?' She approached him suggestively and tried to show him a book. He turned away, thinking it was pornography. It was a book about tomatoes.

'Where's your gorgeous wife, Ken?' Joel, wearing a white-and-green-striped summer suit, was in the room. Ken thought Bunty an even worse tart, seeing that she must have known her husband was outside. He looked at her amazed. Surely Joel couldn't have missed one implication of the scene? Yet he seemed cheerful. 'Where's gorgeous?'

'Lying out in the sun as usual, glorifying her body,' said Ken.

'She's fantastic,' said Joel. Other men were always finding his wife fantastic. He thought he should see a psychiatrist.

'Tell her to use my saloons. Free of charge. Tell her to get together with Bunty. I'm going to get hold of that nightclub artist. I want him to do a trick or two badly, and then have some cornflakes and do it OK. I'll use him in magic slimming as well. I could promote that guy. How's it sound? I've found his agent but I can't find him.'

'Can't you use an actor?' Ken asked. He felt all right with men.

'I've tried actors, but they don't look right. He sort of stayed in my mind. Magic appeal.' He crowed with laughter.

Christine's routine: she woke up feeling unbearably depressed. One 5 mgs Valium, a cigarette, and she stood up. Black coffee, three cigarettes and she could face a bath. Another 5 mgs of Valium and that got Matthew to nursery. Mid-morning she was so down she felt a little smoke might help, so she rolled her first joint. 12 o'clock, first sherry. Lunch, a bottle of wine and a bowl of soup—the soup optional.

Frances thought she was exaggerating.

One day he actually came home at dinner time and she, weak from her routine, was lying on the couch.

'Where's my dinner, Christine?'

She laughed, and when she spoke her voice was slurred. 'I used to do steak and kidney, chicken curry, cheese flan and

135

always by 8.15. And what happened to it? I gave it to the dog.'
She stubbed out the cigarette and lit another one.

He shifted about. The guilt when he did see her made coming into the flat during waking hours a nightmare. 'If you were happy, Christine, you wouldn't smoke so much. It's not good for you.'

Thinking over what she'd been on just that afternoon made her raise her eyes up to the ceiling and laugh.

He gave up drinking after an incident one Saturday afternoon. He was crossing a bridge over the railway line and he saw, in an alley ahead, a middle-aged woman, her skirt up to her waist, slumped lewdly. Feeling he was going to pass out he clung to the rail. There was no one else about. He looked again and saw she was dead. Her head had been battered, there was a scarlet gash from her stomach to her chin, a piece of her clothing was blowing in the wind.

He screamed and then turned and ran. He went down the steps at the end of the bridge three at a time. Then he saw a man crossing the road towards him. He whirled round and at the last minute squeezed into the narrow space between a lamp post and the wall; but the man didn't climb the steps, but carried on up the road, and Ken waited till the footsteps faded. He must get help. He'd get help. The decision was cold, final, and stayed with him as he went back on to the bridge. He'll get help. He approached the body, cautiously, but before he'd even stepped into the alley, he saw that the body was a bundle of old clothing abandoned by the wall, the bloody gash a bright-red scarf holding it together.

He met Jane and she said, 'You look terrible. Thin and fat. You're fat in the gut and thin round the shoulders. Exercise, my boy.'

So he started playing tennis.

Frances thought Ken's problem was blocked creativity, and Christine, watching him shaving one morning, noticed a sudden, disquieting expression. It would rise up in his eyes and then be gone.

'Perhaps you've got blocked creativity. That's why you're so

136

moody.'

'You make it sound like constipation. What's the remedy? Allbran?' And although he laughed he took the idea seriously. It had occurred to him that if he really needed to write music and wasn't doing so, it could be causing the disturbing images and distortion. Giving up alcohol had made no difference. He'd start another opera and work on it full time.

He found Christine in her usual place. 'I'm going to start writing some music. Perhaps an opera.'

She was always solemn before the mirror and, with the arrangement of gold bottles, and flowers and scents, she looked as though she was in front of some altar. 'Oh good.' She was very pleased. She had even turned round.

'I'll do just one more commercial.'

'Why not start the opera now?'

'Because one has to have money to support creative ideas.' He'd also become dependent on the little luxuries. 'I'll start in September. Definitely. The end of September.'

He chose a shirt and tie, and she said, 'If you could be here this evening. Frances is coming to dinner.'

'What for? I didn't know you were friendly with her. Why invite her?'

'She's the only ugly person we know.'

He spun round. 'What a stupid thing to say.'

Her face turned scarlet and she put on three brass bangles. Half the time she was so insecure and drugged she didn't know what she was saying.

'Twitchy poo, darling.'

14

'You carve, Frances. I'll just finish the gravy,' Christine shouted from the kitchen. 'Just one piece for me.'

She hurried in with a bowl of salad. She was wearing a short, low-cut, see-through floral dress and apparently no underclothes. 'Don't trouble about doing it dainty. Just hack it. Ken's hopeless at it. I'm down to 8-5. Isn't it incredible?' Gordon came out of the lavatory, and his eyes popped as he saw her. She sat down and her bosom hung over the low table. Ken closed his eyes. 'Light the candles, poppet,' she told him. 'Oh! The gravy.' She got up and made as much of the movement as she could. Ken sighed.

Gordon, staring uncontrollably, felt he should say something. 'You're very brown.'

'I lie out all day. I'd lie naked if I could, but where is there? I don't wear a bikini, just a very brief black silk bra and matching pants. Men come and lie in a circle around me, like wolves.' She shook her shoulders and the top of her nipples could be seen.

'I'll do it, Fran.' Ken took the long knife and fork and sliced the meat quickly.

'Well, well. He'll do it for you, Frances.'

He threw the fork down, picked up another knife and jabbed at the joint with both knives at once. There was a long silence as everyone watched this peculiar act. Then Christine said, 'That's enough love. We can always have seconds.'

His eyes burned. Yet they were oddly unexpressive. 'Who'd like potatoes?'

Christine had given a lot of thought to hobbies and other topics of conversation since he'd last told her she was bored and boring. She realised contriving an interest in something and talking about it could be disastrous. She couldn't handle politics. She didn't have the education to do much with general knowledge, so she decided to talk about what she did know and was interested in — herself. She'd start with slimming and childbirth.

'So I only gave one push and there was Matthew. It was incredible. The nurses thought it was out of this world.'

There was a long, hysterical silence. Then Gordon and Frances said together, 'Doesn't Christine look — isn't she looking super.'

Ken said, 'Yes.' His smile was sincere. He got up off the floor. 'They've done pretty extensive market research already. Joel wants to deepen the colour of the tins. He says they're not different enough. The slimming jingle's got to go quicker. He wants an overweight dog, its rump dragging on the floor, on the front, and the effect of slimming Snap — i.e. a greyhound — on the back.'

'He's twitched, that guy,' said Christine, clearing the table. 'And that Bunty creature's all boobs and no brains. Has Ken told you his secret?'

'What secret?' they asked.

'I'd better not say. Sorry. Perhaps I've said too much.'

Alarmed, Ken shot up. His dog barked. 'What are you saying?'

Gordon and Frances looked at each other. It was still to early to go home. Christine mouthed the word, 'Opera.'

'Oh that.' He flung himself back on the couch.

'Why get so twitched? Wowee!'

Gordon followed her into the kitchen to help with the coffee.

'I can't stand people prying,' said Ken.

'She wasn't prying,' Frances said, gently.

'Do you feel you want to pry?'

'Of course not.'

'There you are then.' He leaned back and slowly relaxed. Frances, her long hair held off her face by two brown hair-slides, sat by his feet. He felt easy with her. Frances, with her pale, unpainted face, didn't threaten him. Her flesh was unremarkable and covered up. She didn't smell. Her voice was soothing. She would never wiggle. Her desires, if any, were secret and covered by the opaque flesh.

They heard Christine say, 'I always sleep naked between silk sheets.'

'Do you put perfume on them?'

'I put enough on myself, love.' She laughed fiercely. To hear her, Ken thought, you'd never think she was beautiful. Since he'd withdrawn his love she was unanchored and coarse. He grabbed his mineral water.

'Do you miss drinking?' Frances asked.

'I was drinking far too much. I . . . Do you think it could affect your brain?'

'Well, it affects your perceptions.'

'Would the brain damage be irreversible so that symptoms carried on even though you'd stopped?'

'I wouldn't have thought you'd drunk enough for anything like that. What are you worried about? DTs?'

'No, nothing like that,' and he changed the subject.

When she next mentioned his giving up he said he'd done it because he was getting fat.

Christine took Gordon into the bedroom to show him the sheets. Eight lighted Japanese lanterns hung from the ceiling. There was a rubber-plant in one corner, an old antler coat-stand, and a row of old cinema seats against the wall.

'You've done this place really great. You've got such taste.'

It was the first compliment Christine had had in a long time, and for a minute she thought she was going to cry.

'Have you seen your mother?' Frances asked Ken.

'I could see my mother was a lunatic when I was four,' he replied. 'I had to wait till I was fourteen to get away, but I did get away.'

'Does she still push you?'

'Not any more. I push myself. That's enough. My father was rather a sweet person. A bit of an arse-licker but luckily not many people knew, because, as with everything else, my mother had the monopoly on his arse-licking.'

'What does she do now?'

'She overpowers people. Her *au pairs* disappear. I think she eats them. You need to take your entero-vioform with you if you go to dinner up there, I can tell you.'

Christine was in the room, sitting lasciviously on the edge of the steel-rimmed chair. He took no notice of her.

'She likes food with mould on. I think she thinks it's nourishing. I can't stay in the house more than five minutes. I force myself to do twenty. I see her just enough to keep my guilt to a minimum and not enough to let her tear me up. Still, you can't blame your parents. You have a choice.'

'What choice?' asked Christine.

'What you do. What you are.'

'Have you?'

'Of course. Every minute of my life. I don't think I could go on if I didn't.'

'You're lucky,' said Christine.

Frances said, 'So you believe in self-determination?'

'Certainly. What else is there?'

Frances smiled. Smiling, she had an enigmatic, cat-like quality. Christine started finding attractive things about her, but if he'd talked to a dustbin for more than three minutes she'd have found something appealing about the dustbin and got jealous. She writhed on the chair, her long legs mauve-brown in the light. Frances thought that to be as lovely as that must surely mean to be without problems. Even with yellow hair she looked beautiful.

Ken leaned close to Frances as he got his glass of water and said, 'If you marry you'll have a meaningful marriage, Fran. Most people, when they get married, just throw themselves into the slop pail.'

Christine moved quickly. She seemed to leap over the low table. She hit him twice, and then stood breathless with rage, as he cowered, hands covering his head.

She looked as though she was going to spit but turned and went into the bedroom.

Gordon and Frances looked away as he sat up and straightened his tie.

'She's so fucking violent.' He reached for his water, his hand shaking. 'Just an example, Frances, of how meaningful it can get.'

He played tennis with Jane every day. The games were short because she always won, but he spent a lot of time watching her train for the club tournament. She was always asking him to come to dinner, to have lunch, a drink, to meet her husband, but on the other side of a net was how he liked her best.

Jane phoned Christine and talked about a washing-up machine.

'How's Ken's tennis?' Christine asked.

'Uneven. His arms are wishy-washy because his wrists aren't strong. Then suddenly he gets quite a different arm-movement and plays like the fury. He can't keep it up because he doesn't know how he gets it.'

'I suppose he's not consistent about turning up either.'

'He is,' she cried. 'On time too. Come to dinner tomorrow night. Do you know Daniel and Connie? They're coming too. Bring Ken.'

'I'll ask him but he's so incredibly busy.'

He was too incredibly busy.

Ken did go to Jane's club tournament and watched her win the single and mixed doubles. He didn't remember much about it, except that it was very hot and overflowing with boring people. Afterwards, in the clubhouse, kids tore through the piles of cakes and Jane stood close to a short middle-aged Jew and looked flushed, whether from his proximity or sporting success Ken wasn't sure. He went up to a rather plump pretty woman who was pouring lemonade and asked for a drink. She looked sad.

15

Like the dormant stage of an illness it lay low for some months and it wasn't till nearly Christmas time when it started again, violently. Its return coincided with the obligatory twenty minutes in Highgate to see his mother.

'I hear your wife is very thin. Is she ill?'

He dispelled any such hope. 'Slimming. Sorry.' She also wore hornrimmed glasses with plain lenses and sat up in bed reading the dictionary, but he didn't tell her that. He'd clung to Frances, and Christine, clinging to him, had once again changed her image. Frances was insignificant, plain, intelligent and kind. Glasses and the dictionary were the nearest Christine got to it.

'Have a drink.'

'I don't drink.'

'Your father was an alcoholic, among other things.'

'Pack it up. He's dead.'

'But you're not alcoholic. You were breast-fed properly.'

His head swam. He looked out of the window, but her hanging, shrivelled breasts were too ripe an image to escape from.

'You were suckled as often as you wanted—'

'I warn you, Mother. You're making me feel distinctly queasy and I'm not in the mood to be too particular about finding a bog.'

'I'd like my four thousand back.'

'You'll get it.'

'Now.'

'I need it at the moment.'

'I think you made a mistake, Ken. The hanging thing by the front door is a nineteenth-century lantern, not three brass balls.'

'I'm trying to write an opera.'

143

He looked at his watch. Twelve minutes to go. 'They're nice flowers, Mother.'

'You've changed.' Her eyes were baleful. 'I suppose it's that tart.'

'My wife is not a tart.'

'No, you're right, Ken. She'd be all right if she was, but she's only half a tart. A prick-teasing shop-girl on the make. No courage. Don't talk to me about her!' she yelled. 'Get out of my house!'

Eleven minutes. His mother's face was scarlet, her lungs rattled.

'I don't think sending my wife a pair of corsets promoted much good feeling between you,' he said smoothly.

'She's like a cow in rut. All that wriggling and wobbling. She always looks as though she's got at least three tits, and I might add, that's her only distinction. Pour me a drink. Not too much water.'

Ten and a quarter.

'They're almost ripe. Heavy and bright.'

'I asked about your son.'

He shut his eyes. 'I thought you were talking about my tomatoes.' They hung in his mind, fleshy, almost bursting with juice, and they reminded him of something else . . .

'Are you going to put your boy down for Eton?'

. . . Something he shouldn't think about. 'I'm sure we've had this conversation before.' His mind was sticking again. He was sitting down but didn't remember doing so. The images were flitting at the edges of his mind, alien images.

'You don't look well.'

'I'm not sleeping.' They didn't belong to him. He thought he felt hungry and went over to the cake-stand and picked up the long knife.

'Get out of that marriage.'

'It's not possible.'

Suddenly he remembered Christine cutting herself—especially the blood, startling against the pale skin. She'd screamed. There shouldn't have been a scream. Sweating, he moved to the window. He was still holding the knife.

'Get out of it.'

'I can't.'

144

'Of course you can. Especially you. You ought to be used to it.'

Her face had been clenched with pain. He saw it clearly and was surprised that he felt no sympathy. Suddenly he found himself sexually excited. He dropped the knife and pressed his head against the pane of glass. 'I must play tennis. I must play tennis.'

'Can't you keep still, Ken?'

He felt as though he was on fire. Frances' face was white, opaque, and he held it in his mind, held it pressed against the thoughts like a cooling compress.

'Are you going to leave her?'

'I'm trying to make this one work.' Remembering the blood spreading and dripping was a delicious sensation.

'Everyone makes mistakes. The worst one is sticking to something when it's not right for you and you aren't happy.'

'I see you're having a moment of lucidity. Don't tire yourself.' He still had an erection.

'You should choose a partner on your level, emotionally and up here.' She touched her head. 'That girl is slow-witted. No wonder you're not sleeping.'

'Christine is loyal. The marriage will go on and on.'

But in his heart he knew she was right.

'I've got arthritis in my back.' Her voice was harsh. 'Dr Williams says I may have to lie flat for six weeks.'

'How can you lie flat when you're curved over like a boomerang? The man's mad.'

She laughed. 'Come and give mother a kiss.'

He moved further away, clinging to the corner.

'Are you trying to steal a knife?'

'Of course not.' He couldn't remember picking it up again.

'Put it back where it belongs.' She turned her back to show that she trusted him. 'That Nancy girl tried to pinch the spoons. We were twenty to dinner,' and she told him the guest list. If he didn't know it was true he'd have assumed it was another symptom of her lunacy.

Three minutes after the twenty. He'd overstayed.

'Here you are. Christmas present.' She offered him what looked like three pounds. He must be making a mistake. It was usually two.

'Put it on the table.' He didn't want to get near her. Last time he was upset he'd let her get too close and he'd left London.

'Bring me a photo of your boy.'

She was suddenly ill. Her eyes were lopsided and the black irises had run into the whites and were set as though frozen. She should be in an asylum.

He knelt down on his side of the room — he knew this would be difficult — and said softly, 'Why don't you go to a rest home by the sea? I'll fix it up.'

'What are you talking about?' She was amazed. 'I've got half Paris coming next week.'

She came after him to the door — he'd forgotten his Christmas present — and said, 'Get out of it fast. I'll make arrangements for a nanny if you want to keep the child. That woman's making you sick.'

'Mother, I've put a lot into it,' he pleaded. 'It's my last chance to make something work. *She's* put a lot into it.' He was thinking of Christine giving up all those men.

He went home because he was still excited, and he got hold of her, got her into the bedroom, but before he even started making love he knew it wasn't what he wanted. He still felt excited although she left him cold. He couldn't understand it. She cried.

'Is it my past? Is that why you've turned off me?'

'Of course not.' He put his trousers on. 'You know I don't mind about that.'

He rushed out and went back to the narrow streets by the railway line. He got on a local train — he didn't know where he got out, or why. There were gaslamps on the station.

Christine took the eight phials of youth-restorer from the refrigerator and carried them carefully into the bedroom. The sunlamp was on. Her new full-length mirror shone by the window. A towel lay spread on the carpet ready for her floor exercises. Then the phone rang.

She'd spent the autumn trying to find out what he needed. Frances had said, 'A slight relationship. No demands.' And for three days Christine had ignored him. It hadn't made any difference. She'd been light-hearted, and then motherly. She'd tried being independent. She'd gone to Marbella with Matthew for a week and hadn't phoned or written. Unaccountably, sometimes for several hours he wouldn't enter her mind. It was usually when she was doing her beauty regime, but then the joy of those first months would come back to punish her.

She sat on the bed and picked up the phone. Sometimes she believed her heart was actually broken.

Frances said, 'Is he there? He's not shown up, and Joel wants him.'

'No. I've bought some really expensive skin stuff. It's the best in the world. You keep it in the fridge. It costs 80 quid. I was wondering how to break it to him. I really do need it. And Frances, a girl's been killed—murdered so someone said. Connie, that friend of Jane's. In the suburbs somewhere. Very nasty. I'll tell him to ring the studio if I see him. He didn't get back till five this morning. He'd gone out of London to a plant nursery to get something special for his tomatoes.'

Ken went to talk to a priest—he hadn't been in a church since his school days, but he said to Frances 'It's a great relief.' He had his hair cut very short, removed all Christine's more worldly pictures and ornaments, shoved her beauty altar into a far corner, would have put a crucifix above the bed if he hadn't felt it would be ridiculed. He asked her to tone down her appearance. He was fed up with her body.

Christine wore hats and started calling herself Ariel, which badly alarmed Frances. She read poetry and hinted at various artistic circles she was involved in. People said she'd been washing down too many anti-depressants with too much wine.

Yet he stayed with her.

He stood on the highly polished linoleum, under the naked light-bulb, keys warm in his hand. He didn't know where he was. He felt it was night. Then he recognised the lift, the passage and the door of the flat where he lived with Christine. He put the key in the lock and went in.

Chaos. An unaccountably recognisable chaos. Bones and raw flesh on the carpet, a chunk of meat in the corner. Vomit.

Dog shit. 'Yes,' he murmured. 'Yes.' For a moment it gave him indescribable pleasure.

Then he ran, terrified, out of the flat. He stopped before he got to the outer door. He must go back. He must make himself go back.

Christine, alone and as she put it, 'twitched', drank too much. As usual she'd hardly eaten, and the reviving smoke of hash had made her sick. She'd just managed to stagger to bed before she passed out. It was 6 p.m.

Matthew hadn't been put to bed and the dog hadn't been taken out or fed. He'd upset the rubbish and nosed through it for food. Matthew gave him the weekend meat and he'd ravaged it in the living room. Flowers had been knocked over.

Ken came back, and locked and bolted the front door. Matthew, his face tear-stained, was lying by Christine's feet. The cat was washing itself and the dog cowered under a chair. He cleaned it up, all the time muttering, 'Oh God. I'm sorry. I'm sorry.'

'Pick it up, Matt. You know Daddy won't like it.' She recrossed her legs and started swinging them again. She couldn't keep still. 'Isn't he out of this world? He'll break a few hearts, like his Dad.' Her voice was desperately jolly. 'Take the car into the bedroom, precious. He's in all the time now. Doesn't like going out at all. Sometimes he goes out late at night for a walk.'

'Oh Ken,' said Frances. 'I thought you were talking about Matthew.'

Frances' face was full of winter—red nose, blue cheeks, puffy eyes. She sat, thick-skinned, unmoving like a slug.

Christine jumped up and looked in the mirror. Her skirt was slit to the waist and she wore her scarlet skyscrapers. She was so thin her cheeks were hollow and bones stuck out of the top of her chest.

'I've had to watch the drinking. Made a boo-boo the other night. Ariel was a little bit sick. All over the sodding place. I didn't take the dog out as I was high out of my mind, so it piddly-pooed everywhere and ate rubbish. When he came in, he didn't say a word. Just cleared it up.' She grabbed the mirror. 'Is that him?'

148

They listened but no one came in.

'Have to get this out of the way. He can't stand mirrors around the place or clutter. Likes everything bare and clean, as you can see. I always used to hear his footsteps coming along the passage. He's got a distinctive walk. Now I don't hear anything till he puts the key in the lock. He must be wearing rubber soles or something. The hand-washing is getting a bit much. He even sterilises a cup before he uses it. He waits till he thinks I'm not looking. I shudder to think what he does in the lavatory. It makes me and Matt very twitched. D'you know, it was better when he wasn't around so much. I have to think twice before I say anything. I know his success shattered him, but it can't be that any more. The studio's very quiet. It's not blocked creativity either.'

'I've always thought it was his mother,' said Frances. 'But it surprises me he's messed up, because he was such a successful person. He could handle things.'

'He looks different from day to day, hour to hour. I've never seen anyone change so much. He looked dreadful at nine this morning. Said he was too ill to go to the studio, but I saw him in the street at ten looking perfectly healthy. Will you talk to him?'

'Well, it's difficult because I never see him do anything.'

'He behaves all right at the studio?' She was wriggling again.

'Impeccably.'

'I haven't had "it" for a year. Over a year—and I like my bit of pleasure, I can tell you. It's incredible. Now I've started getting obscene phone calls. He doesn't want to know about them. Doesn't want to hear anything like that.' She bent over and picked up a piece of fluff off the carpet.

'Where are the animals?'

'He's put the dog in the kennels. He'll put Matt and me in next. The cat keeps out of his way.'

'Why the hell don't you leave him and go with someone else?' Frances blew her nose, furiously.

Keys chinkled and he was in the flat.

His clothes lacked their usual elegance. His behaviour was unassuming. He said he was pleased to see Frances, and they drank tea.

'Are you better?' Frances asked, as Christine furtively moved the mirror.

'Why do you ask?' His eyes gleamed.

'Well, you said this morning you were ill.'

'Well, people can get better, can't they? Or is that a crime?' His voice was soft.

'Not in half an hour,' said Christine.

'Half an hour? I was lying down all day. I went out for some fresh air just before you got in with Matthew.'

'I saw you in the street, love, not twenty minutes after you said you were too ill to move.'

His eyes shifted, avoided theirs. 'It couldn't have been me. Definitely not.' He looked up and smiled, a brilliant smile. 'You wear so much muck on your eyes you can hardly see out of them.'

'Anyway,' said Frances, giving Christine a meaningful look, 'if you skive off for a few hours and do Joel down—who cares? You've worked like hell for him. He's upset because he's had to abandon his magical cornflakes. He knows where the magician lives—North London somewhere—but he's avoiding Joel. Won't answer letters, telegrams or phone calls.'

They sat quietly, but it was not a pleasant silence. Neither Frances nor Christine could think what to say. He spun round to Christine. 'What's wrong now?'

'Nothing.' She was taken aback. 'I was just thinking about Christmas.'

They went on sitting quietly. Christine could see him looking at her arm, and all of a sudden it gave her a funny feeling. Yet she couldn't draw the arm in, and it lay stranded along the back of the couch.

Then he smiled, widely. 'Joel's thinking of doing a cat-food and a bird-food along the lines of Snap. We'll get a sensational contract.'

'What about the opera?' asked Frances.

'I can't really get into it because of all the ads.'

'All what ads?' she asked.

'Well, it's the thought of them.'

'That murdered girl was buried today,' said Christine. 'No one knows what happened.'

'Do I have to hear all that again?' He went into the bedroom and changed his shirt.

'How's your mother?' Frances asked when he came back.

There was a nasty hush, and Frances, ignoring Christine's warning look — Mother was one of the dodgy subjects — said, 'Are you going there for Christmas?'

'Nope.'

'I thought you always went for Christmas lunch?'

'I don't see her, actually. She's catching.' He turned and looked at Frances, his eyes wide. He had nothing to hide. 'She's very sick and she makes me feel uncomfortable. She'll manage. She'll have to be responsible for herself just as everyone else should be.'

He emptied Frances's ashtray into the new wicker basket and then emptied the basket into the kitchen rubbish bin. He came back with a wet cloth and wiped the inside of the ashtray. Frances felt she should resist another cigarette. Discreetly, Christine took a Valium. Ken left the room.

'Washing his hands, I bet,' whispered Christine. 'I can't ask you to stay to dinner because he wouldn't — ' Matthew came out of the bedroom and climbed into Christine's lap. 'That poor girl who was done in had four kids apparently. What will happen to them? I must phone Jane.'

Frances looked for her coat. He'd hung it up.

'He won't allow Wendy or Pat in the place after Wendy told a joke about a dog with sexual problems. Actually the joke was rather good. A man goes into the — '

Frances turned round. 'I thought he was in the room.'

'He was,' she whispered. 'He's gone again.'

Christine wondered if he'd committed a crime. She hadn't forgotten the way he ran away outside the shop in Kensington. He was always disappearing, reappearing.

Then she realised that what was wrong with him was much worse than that.

16

Christine hated going outside because, still convinced that Ken
wanted other women, she was tortured by every attractive
woman she saw. Fat ones, short ones, long glamourous
ones—even plain ones—there were so many he could fancy.

Ken hated going outside because he felt threatened by
women.

He fired Gordon. It was impossible to know if Ken was in the
conservatory or not, as the plants were so plentiful and thick,
and one morning Gordon, thinking he was alone, made a
phone call.

'He's a cunning bastard. Slippery. I wouldn't trust him. It's
nothing you can pin down.'

It was with amazement that Ken realised that Gordon was
talking about him.

He fired him because Gordon discovered the letter. On
impulse Ken had written an anonymous letter to the *News of
the World* which could only be described as boastful. Writing
in red ink, he had extolled his success in the raising of tomatoes
and added that he would never be caught. At the bottom, a
PS: *'I'm a runner. Ha Ha.'*

The sealed note was laid ready to post. Gordon had opened
it and read it. It had meant nothing to him and he'd resealed
it. Ken peering, between two tomato plants, had seen him.

Frances was allowed one more visit to the flat—she'd
brought a present for Matthew. It was cold outside, but inside
the atmosphere was icy. Christine seemed to have reached a
crisis of beautified sex appeal. She strutted and glittered like
some exotic bird.

In the corner of the dust-free room sat Ken, morose,
dull-eyed—his sterilised cup in front of him, the carpet freshly
groomed.

152

Christine bent over, revealed knickers which were no more than a strip of black lace, wiped the clean table, dried it and put his dinner of boiled rice, raw vegetables and an apple in front of him. She was still sunburnt. The television was off, but Matthew still sat in his usual viewing place, staring, his hands full of bricks.

'Ken bought me a marvellous present.' Her voice was hushed. 'Come and look.' She took Frances into the bedroom. Lying across the bed was an ankle-length white fur-coat. Tenderly she picked it up. 'Isn't it too incredibly—Ken is so fantastically—It's going to be a sensational Christmas.' She put the coat on. 'I feel I'm on the edge of a volcano.'

The lanterns had been taken down and the beauty altar was out of sight.

Ken finished his dinner and peeled his apple, carefully.

'Out of this world,' said Christine for no reason, as she took his plate and cup into the kitchen. He wiped the table with a paper tissue. Then he saw the coat.

'You're not going out?'

She mistook his worried tone, thought he was being unusually protective until she said, 'Why not?' and he replied, 'Because it's dark.'

Two sets of eyes were looking at him and they contained the same expression. Uneasily, he got up.

'The only thing is to do what you believe in. Commit yourself. It's the only answer,' he said hoping to placate those eyes.

'What—Snap, you mean?' said Christine. 'So you have signed the new contract.'

'Without it there would be no point.' He looked at Frances, his eyes bright. 'God is the only thing that makes sense. You can see that.'

'I'm glad,' said Frances.

He walked up and down in front of them, almost swaggering, and she was reminded of the letter.

'Did you get rid of Gordon because he opened that letter?'

He stood still, hands in his pockets, looking innocent. 'Letter?'

'The one he opened. He told me it was to a newspaper. About tomatoes.'

153

'Oh that.' He laughed. 'Of course not. The letter was a joke.'

'Gordon's very hurt. Why didn't you at least see him and let him apologise? You can't amputate people. I don't believe in amputating people.'

His eyes, as he stared at her, were feverish. Then he smiled, a warm caressing one. 'Of course I'll see him, Frances.'

They played cards. The cat came out of some furniture and curled round Frances' shoulder, purring loudly. It dug her in the cheek, playfully, and the paw made a dent. The flesh, instead of springing back, stayed dented. Ken stared, horrified.

'The nine, Ken. I've played the nine.'

Without speaking he went into the bathroom and locked the door.

Christine was suprised to hear him call urgently. He unlocked the door and pulled her in. 'Get her out!'

She looked amazed. 'What's she done?'

'Get her out. Out!'

'What d'you mean? I can't. She's bought a present for Matt and we're playing cards. It was your idea.'

'She goes or I go.' He gripped her shoulder painfully.

'All right, Ken.'

He stayed in the lavatory till she'd got rid of Frances.

Later he said, 'You saw her flesh. You must have. If you press it, your fingers go right in and the flesh doesn't spring back. Her flesh is decaying.'

'Oh don't keep going on about it. Don't exaggerate. She's just sluggish.'

Christine was left with her perfect body which she could only pamper and look at. Ken was stranded with terrible impulses he couldn't understand. He became meek. Sometimes Christine thought she'd rather the volcano erupted than that they go on like this. They got through Christmas.

17

It was the New Year. He sat on the bed and looked at his hands. He looked at them as though they were to blame. The phone rang again. Bunty said, 'Shall I come round?'

'No. No. That's the last thing I want.'

'I want to talk to you . . .'

'Talk to Joel.'

'He laid me on the bed, spread my legs, put my arms above__'

'You disgusting bitch!'

'Well, thank you very much! I was only trying to help you.'

It was nearly dark and the flat was oppressive.

'Fatboy is disgusting.' She laughed. *'Actually, I'd quite like it with the right person.'*

He looked at his hands again. They were filling up, they were hungry. He crushed a matchbox and it gave him pleasure.

'Fatboy can't get it together unless it's perverted.'

'You're a cow! Why do you tell me such disgusting things? I've got my own problems.' He put the phone down. It was dark.

There was some spilt powder on the dressing table. Stockings lay tangled by the window. The plants were upturned. A nail-varnish bottle, its top off, lay on its side, and the scarlet stuff had crawled out and almost reached the edge, when its escape had been cut off by oxygen. The full-length mirror was cracked. She hadn't taken the white fur.

'Violent bitch!'

The phone rang. 'Perhaps you're frightened.'

'Not if I can keep moving.'

'One night stands, eh?'

'I was talking about travel.'

'Perhaps you like what's out of reach?'

'I only like what's out of reach.'

Fatboy whipped me last night. Tonight it'll be the other way round. He wants me to dress up. I just think of you.' She was breathless.

'I don't want to hear about it.'

'I'm coming—'

'Shut up!'

'. . . over—cheer you up . . .'

When he woke up, the street was silent. Deadly silence of the middle of the night. The cat was slipping across the dressing table.

The phone rang. Bunty said, *'I love you.'*

He put the phone down and sat on the edge of the bed, head in hands. He supposed he wanted something. A pee? The light on? A cigarette? He must need a cigarette.

The phone rang again. He left it off the hook and started to shake.

Everything was closing in.

18

He went back to the conservatory, and the feel of the lovely smooth tomatoes calmed him. The leaves were cool.

She came in quietly. The conservatory light winked and glistened and made her look flashy.

'Come and sit in the studio. It's warmer.' That got her out of there.

'I wondered how you were?'

He shrugged. 'How's Matthew?'

She sat at the tapes table. On it, the remains of his breakfast — a greasy plate, a knife, a fork, an apple. She stabbed her cigarette out on the plate. 'Are you eating here?'

'I did this morning. I couldn't face the flat.' He locked sideways at his conservatory, all the windows filled with ripe tomatoes.

'You're in your own skin, Ken. That's what's wrong with you.' Her lips were overpainted. 'I need money.' She crossed her legs and the short coat fell away and her thighs gleamed. She leant back provocatively. 'It is my past you disapprove of, isn't it?'

'Who am I to disapprove? I didn't like it because it harmed you, but that's over.'

In the days when she had lots of men she'd looked plump and comforting. She hadn't made love for a year and she looked like a whore. He offered her another cigarette and wished she'd go away.

'You're so fussy. A prig. I'd never have thought it, Matt's so upset he craps himself. Has for ages, but I didn't think I should tell you.'

Ken closed his eyes.

'Of course he senses everything's wrong,' she said.

'Everything isn't wrong, Christine,' he said gently. He shook his head, gestured with his hands, tried to speak. 'Unfamiliar things seem familiar '

157

'Have you done something wrong?'

She didn't like the way he turned, the look in his eye. 'I mean, you keep disappearing in crowds.'

'If I don't like crowds, is that a crime?'

'No. But you behave as though you're guilty. It's the only way to explain it.'

He could see the flesh then — globular, orange. His mind was full of it. It was flooded with blood.

'Why say you were at Joel's when you were in the conservatory? What's the reason? Tell me.'

'I keep seeing flesh.'

'Well, that's all right. We all do.'

'No. The inside flesh, under the skin.'

'Have you ever seen a road accident?'

'No.'

'You must have and forgotten.'

'I'm haunted, by all sorts of things.' He looked with longing at the conservatory. 'I think I'd be better on my own. For a while.'

This wasn't what she expected. She started crying.

'I can't cope, Christine. You can see that.'

He went behind her and bent slightly. His lips touched her hair, tenderly. He put his arm round her. It slipped up against her neck. Then he saw the knife. Then he understood what he wanted.

Her fingers were grappling with his arm.

He jumped away, over to the other side of the studio.

'Christ, Ken. You hurt my neck. You don't have to squeeze me that hard.'

'I'm sorry. Sorry. I'm sorry.'

'You said I had stamina. That's the only compliment you've paid me for a long time, but it's not true. I need love.'

'Go on, let me,' said the coarse voice. *'Let me do it to you, pretty boy. You'll like it.'*

'You know that,' said Christine. 'You know how much I longed for you in bed. Christ, we were doing it all the time. It was like the first time for me. I've never had anything like it.'

'I'll do it free. It's my speciality.'

'Shut up!' he screamed.

'Of course everyone knows. Frances told me to frig myself.

How does that make you look?'

He rushed towards her and grabbed the knife. The greasy steel glinted magnificently.

'No!' she shrieked.

'Put it into me, big boy.' Harsh cigarette cough.

Holding the knife down by his side he walked quickly into the conservatory and shut the door.

There was silence.

'Ken!'

Then a low animal moan and something red shot against the glass. For a moment Christine thought it was tomato juice. It gushed down the window, dark and rich. A hoarse shriek and more blood splashed against the opposite side. A loud crash, glass tinkled. Tomatoes, sliced, hacked, plopped against the windows, against the roof. More burst, their juice mingling with the blood and chopped flesh. Long shattered sounds, glass crashing, hideous screams. The noise was deafening. He'd almost destroyed the conservatory. Then there was a last tremendous crash as he fell through the jagged glass and half lay among the mess of tomatoes, ripped to pieces.